Black-Eyed Devils

Catrin Collier's mother was a Prussian refugee and her father was Welsh. She has published over twenty historical novels and eight crime novels (under the name Katherine John).

Her first historical novel, Hearts of Gold, was filmed as a mini series by BBC Worldwide. It starred David Warner, Judy Parfitt and Kate Jarman and attracted an audience of 6.8 million viewers.

Catrin has an adult education centre named after her in Pontypridd, the Welsh valleys town where she was born. She lives with her family on the coast near Swansea.

Black-Eyed Devils

Published by Accent Press Ltd – 2009

ISBN 9781906373610

The Quick Reads project in Wales is a joint venture between Basic Skills Cymru and the Welsh Books Council. Titles are funded through Basic Skills Cymru as part of the National Basic Skills Strategy for Wales on behalf of the Welsh Assembly Government.

Printed and bound in the UK

Cover design by The Design House

Sgiliau Sylfaenol
Basic Skills
Cymru

Black-Eyed Devils

Catrin Collier

ACCENT PRESS LTD

Chapter One

'Straight down to the picket line at the colliery and straight back, Amy. No stopping to talk to anyone,' Mary Watkins warned her daughter.

Amy's blue eyes shone with mischief. 'It would be rude to ignore the neighbours if they talked to me, wouldn't it, Mam?'

Mary tried not to smile. 'Don't look at me as if you don't know what I'm talking about, my girl. Stay away from the soldiers and police.'

Amy wrinkled her nose. 'You don't have to tell me to stay away from the soldiers and police. Father Kelly says there'll soon be more officers in Tonypandy than colliers. And all the police do is watch the picket lines. You'd think they have better things to do. Like catch thieves.'

'The only places worth thieving from these days are the pawn shops. There are more goods behind their counters than in our houses.' Mary watched Amy tease curls out from under her bonnet. 'I'll add Father Kelly's nephew to that list of men you should stay away from.'

'I hardly know Tom Kelly.'

'You know him well enough to spend hours talking to him when you're supposed to be working in the soup kitchen.'

'Who's been gossiping to you?' Amy asked.

'People who are concerned about you,' Mary answered.

'People should mind their own business,' Amy replied. 'Besides, Tom Kelly's only been in Tonypandy a week.'

'That's long enough for some men. What has he been telling you?'

'About Ireland. It sounds like a beautiful country.'

'He might have been telling you about Ireland, but he's on his way to America.'

'I know, he told me that too.'

'So, don't get interested in a man who'll only be in Tonypandy for a couple of weeks. You'll get hurt if you do, Amy,' Mary warned.

Amy could no more stop thinking about Tom Kelly than she could stop breathing. That didn't stop her from giving her mother the reply Mary expected. 'Yes, Mam.'

Mary poured cold tea from the teapot through a strainer into an enamel jug. 'Fill the men's cans for me, love. I'll prepare the tea leaves for drying. They can go in the oven when we light the fire tonight. It'll be their third brew, but it's all the tea we'll have until the next strike pay.'

Amy lifted down her father's and brothers' "snap" cans from the dresser. She filled them with cold tea and screwed on the tops. 'Do you want me to take them anything besides this?'

'Like what? The hens haven't laid today and the cupboards are empty.' Mary tried not to sound bitter. It was a woman's job to keep her family fed, clean and warm. She hated not being able to put a good meal in front of her husband and grown sons when they returned from their shifts on the picket. And, no matter how much she and Amy cut back on their share, there was never enough food for the six-year-old twins. Sam's and Luke's eyes had grown large in their thin faces. They hadn't had the energy to go out to play after school for months.

As a union man's wife, Mary had been one of the first women in the town to agree that the strike was necessary. The miners had no choice but to withdraw their labour when management refused their request for a decent wage. But watching her children go hungry was almost more than she could bear.

Amy smiled. 'The cupboards aren't empty.'

'What have you been up to?' Mary was worried. Her eldest son, Jack, worked in the illegal drift mines the men had opened up on the mountain. Without the miners' free ration of coal, there was no fuel to heat water or houses, or to cook what little food they had. The men insisted that the coal that came out of the drifts was essential and worth the risk. But if Jack was caught, he would be fined. A fine meant prison because they had no savings left.

Amy opened the cupboard and lifted out a cake tin. She opened it and showed her mother the contents. 'There are twelve in here.'

'Welsh cakes? Wherever did you get them?'

'I helped make them in the soup kitchen this morning after I cleaned the vegetables. Mrs Evans persuaded Mr Hopkin Morgan, the baker, to donate the ingredients but he didn't give her any dried fruit.'

'At the price it is that's not surprising. It was good of him to give her the flour, sugar and margarine. What did you use to mix them?'

'Water, a little milk, and three of the eggs the colliers who keep hens donated. Father Kelly's housekeeper gave us the last of her home-made jam to fill them. Mrs Evans insisted I take these for helping.'

'Leave them here,' Mary said. 'Your father won't eat them in front of the other men and twelve cakes won't give them a bite each. We'll have one each tonight and keep the last four for the twins' breakfast tomorrow.'

Amy returned the tin to the cupboard and packed the cans of cold tea into her basket.

'Straight down and back,' her mother reminded her. 'And, when you go to the soup kitchen this afternoon, take the jug and the last shilling from the strike pay and get it filled. There's no bread left so it will be just soup tonight.' Mary drained the teapot into a bowl and tipped the tea leaves on to a baking tray.

'Do you want me to get anything else while I'm in town, Mam?' Amy lifted down the cloak she shared with her mother. As hers was almost new, it had been one of the first things to be pawned when the men had come out on strike.

'I'll have ten of everything they're giving away free.' The joke was used by every miner's wife in the Rhondda.

Amy didn't find it funny. 'Won't be long.' Amy kissed her mother, walked down the passage, opened the front door and left the house. Although it was late September, the winter rains had come early. Most of the women in the street were outside, scrubbing their front steps with stones and cold water because they couldn't afford soap. Outdoors was wetter but no colder than their unheated stone houses.

'You going down the picket line, love?' Enyd Jenkins who lived opposite the Watkins's asked Amy.

'Yes, Auntie Enyd. I was about to call in. Would you like me to take Uncle Gwilym's tea down for him?'

'If you don't mind, love. I've got his can ready and it will save me a walk. I promised to go to the soup kitchen early to organise things for Father Kelly. He called in to tell me that he has to go out on parish business. Come in.'

Amy followed Enyd into her house and up the stone-flagged passage to the kitchen. It was as clean, bare and cold as her mother's.

Enyd handed her the can. 'Tell Gwilym I'm sorry I have nothing more to give him.'

'I will.' Amy dropped it into her basket with the others.

'And mind how you go.'

'You're as bad as Mam, Auntie Enyd.' Amy had known Enyd all her life. She was her mother's closest friend and had moved to Tonypandy from Pontypridd at the same time as her parents. 'Mam's given me the full lecture. No talking to soldiers or policemen.'

'Or Tom Kelly?' Enyd watched Amy carefully.

'Was it you who told Mam we'd been talking to one another in the soup kitchen?'

'If I did, it's only because I'm worried about you, love.'

'It's as bad as having two mothers watching my every step. I'm a grown woman.'

'You're nineteen, Amy, and I remember what I was like at your age. Silly and headstrong. It's easy to make a mistake that can ruin your life.'

'I know Tom Kelly's on his way to America, if that's what you're concerned about.'

'From what I've heard, he can't afford to take himself, let alone baggage like you.' Enyd followed Amy back down the passage. 'And look out for blacklegs. There's going to be trouble. Whatever you do, don't get caught up in any fighting.'

'I won't be seeing any blacklegs, Auntie Enyd. They stay behind the police line inside the colliery.'

Enyd lowered her voice when she reached

her doorstep. 'My Gwilym's heard that management's been bringing them into the town for the last two weeks. They're hiding them among the soldiers in the lodging houses. It's best you avoid all strangers, Amy.'

'I will.'

'You're not cross with me for telling your mother about Tom Kelly?'

Amy shook her head. She could never be angry with her Auntie Enyd. Not for long. 'I know you're only thinking of me.' She kissed her aunt's cheek. 'Bye, Auntie Enyd.'

Enyd watched Amy until she turned the corner. Despite so little food and the constant rain, there was a spring in Amy's step. Enyd suddenly remembered what it felt like to be young. Not that she had ever been as pretty as Amy Watkins.

Tall, slender with silver blonde hair and deep blue eyes, Amy had attracted admiring looks since her fifteenth birthday. When she'd caught her husband, Gwilym, watching Amy, he'd said, "Enyd, I might be nearer fifty than forty, but I still recognise beauty when I see it. And Amy Watkins has something of the same look about her that you had when we married fifteen years ago."

Enyd had been upset by the comparison.

But she had been careful not to shed her tears in front of Gwilym.

Father Kelly hailed Amy as soon as she stepped into Dunraven Street. The Catholic priest tugged at the sleeve of the young man with him and ran across the road to meet her. It took them a few minutes to avoid a procession of women who were carrying a rag and straw dummy of Arnold Craggs, a director of the Glamorgan colliery. The women were taking it in turns to whack the dummy with carpet beaters.

'Good day to you, Amy,' the priest greeted her. 'Hope the world is treating you and your family well. We'll be seeing you at the soup kitchen later?'

'You will, Father.'

'Tom.' He pulled the young man forward. 'Aren't you going to say hello to the prettiest girl in Wales?'

'When you let me get a word in, Uncle.'

'It's Father, Tom.' Father Kelly was enjoying teasing his nephew. From the moment Tom had stepped into St Gabriel and Raphael's church hall a week ago, he hadn't looked at anything or anyone except Amy Watkins. Every chance Tom had he worked with Amy.

When they weren't working, they were sitting in corners talking. Every kitchen helper had noticed.

'I'm not the prettiest girl in Wales, Father.' Amy kissed the priest's cheek. Her family were Baptist, but everyone in town, Anglican, Chapel or Salvation Army, loved Father Kelly. The day the strike had been declared he'd opened a soup kitchen, turning his church hall into a canteen. Whenever help was needed, he was always first on the scene. And he never spoke of religion outside the church unless someone asked him to.

'As if an Irishman or priest would lie about a woman's beauty.' Father Kelly slipped his arm around Amy's shoulders and hugged her. 'Amy, darling, just look at the effect you're having on my brother's son. Young Tom Kelly.'

Amy smiled at Tom and Tom smiled back at her. Amy's mouth went dry. Tom seemed even more handsome outdoors than he had been in the kitchen. Her three older brothers were all over six feet. "Young Tom Kelly" was at least four inches taller. He had the same thick curly hair as his uncle. The priest's was iron grey, Tom's blue-black and glossy. His eyes were dark and they gleamed like wet coal when he offered her his hand.

'The morning's all the better for seeing you, Miss Watkins.'

Amy was aware of the warmth of Tom's fingers when they closed over hers. The lilt of his voice, the fresh, clean smell of wind and rain that clung to the shabby tweed suit that was too small for him. But most of all she was aware of the warmth of his body as he stood next to her. And of her own face, mirrored in his eyes.

'You do know Tom's only here for a week or two,' the priest said. 'He's on his way to America.'

'He told me.' Amy answered.

'As I've been telling Miss Watkins, America is a grand land with lots of opportunity for a hard-working man, Uncle.'

'Father,' Father Kelly corrected.

'And I've relations out there who'll see me all right.' Tom continued to stare at Amy.

'We'd best move on, Amy, Tom.' Father Kelly nudged his nephew. He'd spotted one of the London policemen who'd been sent into Tonypandy.

The officer walked up to them. 'You're blocking the pavement, Father Kelly.'

'Sorry, Constable, it's my nephew. He doesn't want to leave Miss Watkins. He's never seen a girl as pretty as her before.'

The constable didn't understand the priest's joke. He studied Amy as if she was a piece of meat on a butcher's slab.

Amy shivered.

'Your father a miner?' he demanded.

'Yes.' Amy lifted her chin. Her father had ordered everyone in the family to avoid the soldiers and the police who had been sent into the town to keep order after the strike had begun. But he'd also told them not to treat the officers with more respect than they did any other man.

'Yes, what?'

'Yes, Constable.' Amy knew he wanted her to call him "Sir". In her opinion, the only difference between him and other men was the uniform he was wearing.

'What's your father's name?'

'James Watkins.'

'Jim Watkins, the strike leader?'

'He's an organiser,' Amy said.

'You've three brothers. Jack, Mathew and Mark?'

She was worried about where his questions were leading, but she tried not to show fear. 'I have.'

Tom Kelly gave her hand a reassuring

squeeze. Father Kelly drew closer to her.

'Warn Jack, he'd better behave himself. He's been seen digging in the illegal mines on the mountain. One day we're going to catch him at it and then he'll be sorry.' The officer pointed at her with his index finger.

The crowd that had gathered around them fell silent when Tom caught the officer's hand in mid-air. He held it fast.

'Where I come from we don't insult a lady by poking her, Constable,' Tom said quietly. 'I think you should put your other hand in your pocket. Then I suggest you apologise to Miss Watkins.'

Chapter Two

A loud crash broke the silence that had fallen over the street. Startled, Amy turned and saw some men unloading wooden barrels from a brewer's cart. They were rolling them down a ramp and into the cellar of the White Hart. The striking colliers might not have any money for beer, but the soldiers and police who had been brought in to control them did.

'You Irish,' the constable spat in disgust. 'You're nothing but troublemakers, the lot of you.' He unhooked his four foot truncheon from his belt with his free hand and raised it in front of Tom's face.

'What's the problem here, Constable Shipton?' Sergeant Martin, a local police officer, had pushed towards them through the crowd.

'This Irishman assaulted me, sir.'

Angry murmurs rose from the people. Constable Shipton lowered his truncheon after a signal from the sergeant. Tom finally let go of the officer's hand.

'Did you assault Constable Shipton, Mr ...?'

'Thomas Kelly, Sergeant. No, I did not assault Constable Shipton. I grabbed his hand because he was about to poke the lady.'

'Poke the lady?' Sergeant Martin repeated. 'Were you about to assault Miss Watkins, Shipton?'

'I didn't touch her, sir.'

'Only because I grabbed his hand, preventing him,' Tom said.

'I was giving Miss Watkins a warning to pass on to one of her brothers,' Constable Shipton said. 'He was seen working in an illegal drift mine on the mountain, sir.'

'By you, Constable Shipton?'

'By an informer, sir.'

The crowd moved restlessly. Voices rose in anger. Hundreds of miners had been imprisoned on the evidence of "anonymous informers". No one could be sure whether the informers were real or if the police simply made up the evidence. As a result, Tonypandy had changed from a friendly town to a place where people distrusted their neighbours.

Everyone knew that the authorities would pay two shillings for the name of a striker who had attacked a blackleg, as strike breakers were called. The price for betraying a miner who worked in a drift mine was a shilling.

'If you have proof that Jack Watkins has been working in an illegal drift mine, why haven't you taken him into custody?' Father Kelly asked the constable. 'Wouldn't that be more sensible than threatening his sister as she goes about her lawful business? Or are the police targeting the miners' women now, because they are too afraid to speak to the men?'

'It's not police policy to target women, Father.' Sergeant Martin turned to the crowd. 'All of you move on. You know it's illegal to gather in the street.'

'We were trying to move on, Sergeant Martin,' Father Kelly protested. 'Constable Shipton stopped us.'

'He's not stopping you now, Father.'

'Thanks to you, Sergeant.' The priest took Amy's arm and walked on, leaving Tom to follow.

'I have to cross the road, Father.' Amy stopped opposite Rodney's, the grocer's shop. 'I'm taking my father and brothers their tea. They're picketing the Glamorgan Colliery.'

'You could find more trouble down there

than you have here,' the priest said.

'I have to go. Dad's on a twelve-hour shift. My brothers are taking it in turns to keep him company. They need something to drink.'

'I'd go with you, but Mrs Edwards has sent for me. The poor woman is not long for this world.'

'I'll walk Miss Watkins to the picket,' Tom said.

'You don't know Tonypandy, Tom. When a man is seen "walking out" with a girl, the gossips will have them engaged in a week and married in two.'

'I'll risk the gossip if Miss Watkins will.' Tom winked at Amy.

Amy's heart started pounding rapidly again. She would love to "walk out" with Tom. But the last thing she wanted was for Father Kelly and Tom to think she couldn't look after herself. 'I've been walking to the picket for months without any bother from anyone, Father.'

'I know you have. I also know that, as my nephew here isn't a collier or a policeman, both sides will distrust him.'

Tom wasn't to be put off so easily. 'They'll not be throwing stones at a man who hasn't taken sides.'

'It's obvious from your cap and clothes, boy, you're a working man. That puts you on the side of the colliers.'

'There's no need for you to walk me, Mr Kelly,' Amy said.

'I'd appreciate someone showing me more sights of Tonypandy than my uncle has been able to. As for the gossips, I am Father Kelly's nephew.'

'But you're not a priest.'

'No, I'm not. Nor will I ever be.' He laughed.

Father Kelly saw that Tom was determined to stay with Amy. He also saw Constable Shipton watching them again. It was time they moved on. 'You'll be safe enough with Tom, Amy. As long as you can keep him from arguing with any more police officers.'

'I promise, no arguing with anyone unless they threaten Miss Watkins. I'll see you back at the soup kitchen, Uncle.' Tom offered Amy his arm.

'As you've promised not to pick any more quarrels, Mr Kelly, I accept your offer to walk me to the picket line.' Amy's cheeks burned when she linked her arm in Tom's. She was embarrassed. She hadn't blushed since she was a child.

'You know that young Irishman, Father?'

Sergeant Martin walked up to Father Kelly after Tom had led Amy across the road.

'Tom's my nephew. My dead brother's son. God rest his soul.' The priest crossed himself.

'Strange time for him to come visiting you, the middle of the strike.'

'His mother died a month ago. He came to say goodbye. There's nothing to keep him in the old country. He's decided to try and make his fortune in America.'

'He won't be staying with you long?'

'Give the boy chance to catch his breath, Sergeant. He only arrived in town a week ago.'

'I'll give him a chance to catch his breath and say goodbye to you, Father. I won't give him time to meet with any of the other Irishmen who have suddenly appeared in Tonypandy. Do I need to explain why?'

'No.' Father Kelly shook his head. 'I'm ashamed to admit that some of my countrymen have decided to turn blackleg. It upsets me that they're helping Arnold Craggs and the colliery management to try and break the strike.'

Sergeant Martin softened his voice. 'There are Welsh as well as Irish blacklegs, Father.'

'Desperate men, all of them, whose only

concern is to feed their families. I must be off, Sergeant.' The priest lifted his hat. 'My regards to your wife.'

'I'll pass them on, Father. And I'll try to control my officers. Some of the men they've brought up from London, like Constable Shipton, are more hot-headed than we locals.'

'I've noticed. Good day to you, Sergeant.'

'Were you born in Tonypandy?' Tom couldn't stop looking at Amy. His uncle had been joking when he'd told Constable Shipton that Tom had never seen anyone like Amy before. But it was the truth. Tom had to stop himself from reaching out and touching the strands of silver hair that fell over Amy's shoulders from beneath her bonnet. Her eyes were the brightest, clearest blue he'd ever seen. When she spoke, the Welsh lilt in her voice sounded like music.

'My parents moved here from Pontypridd a few weeks before I was born. My father was offered a better job with more pay in the Glamorgan Colliery than he'd been earning in the Maritime. He's a repairer.' Amy wanted Tom to know that her father was no ordinary collier. 'It's his job to maintain the airways in the pit, check they are kept clear and that the air below ground is good quality.'

'An important job.'

'It is. My eldest brother, Jack, is his assistant.'

'How old is Jack?'

'Why do you want to know?'

'The constable said you've three brothers. I'd like to know how many grown men I have to fight off when I come to get you.'

'Why would you want to "get me"?' she asked warily.

'To carry you off to my castle. Isn't that what knights in shining armour do when they find the damsel they want to marry?'

'Marry?' she repeated. 'That's very funny considering we only met for the first time a few days ago.'

'I've thought of nothing but you since.'

'Have you indeed?'

'Have you thought of me?'

'No,' she lied.

'Like me, you must have known that we were meant for one another the moment you saw me. So, why fight your feelings?'

'The only thing I felt the first time I saw you was a cold wind blowing in through the church hall door.'

'No you didn't. You felt the scorching warmth of my love.'

'I'm used to Father Kelly's funny Irish way of talking, but you take it too far.'

He dropped his joking tone. 'I'm serious, Amy. I will marry you, you'll see. And you haven't answered my question. How old are your brothers?'

'Jack's twenty-two, Mathew twenty-one and Mark twenty. Mathew and Mark work as carpenters in the coal pit. I've two younger brothers as well. They're twins. Sam and Luke are six years old.'

'I'm guessing you're eighteen.'

'You'd guess wrong. I'm nineteen.'

'The perfect age for marriage to a man of twenty-three.'

She ignored his last remark. 'Have you any brothers and sisters?'

'One brother and nine sisters, all older than me. Eight of the girls are married. Bridget went into a convent.'

'As a nun?'

'It's better than going in as a maid of all work. The girls knew one of them would have to join the church. Bridget volunteered. Every generation of my family has its priests and nuns. My brother Peter's a priest, like my uncle.

He's in America. It was his letters about the opportunities there that gave me the idea of emigrating.'

'What are you going to do when you get there?'

'Work.'

'At what?'

'I'll be able to answer that question for you when I see what I'm offered.'

'You'd like to write to me?' she asked.

'No, take you with me. You will come?'

'Look! There's Dad. Over there.' Amy was glad she had an excuse not to answer him.

Amy was used to young men asking her to go for a walk with them. She knew how to reject them without hurting their feelings. She'd also slapped three boys for trying to steal kisses from her. But Tom Kelly with his talk of marriage wasn't like any man she'd ever met. He made her feel oddly uneasy.

Strangest of all, she couldn't understand why she didn't want to send him away from her just yet.

Amy ran towards her father. He and the other striking miners had pinched an old oil drum. They'd punched holes in the sides to turn it into a brazier, and were burning scraps of wood and wooden pit railings to keep warm.

'I've brought your tea, Dad. Uncle Gwilym's too.' Amy took the tins from her basket and handed them out.

'Who's the man?' Jim Watkins eyed Tom warily.

Tom stepped forward and held out his hand. 'Tom Kelly, sir.'

'A Black-Eyed Devil.'

'A what?' Tom asked in confusion.

'It's what the colliers call Irish blacklegs,' Amy whispered.

Jim's face darkened in anger. 'Look at Amy again and you'll go back to Ireland in a box.'

'Dad, Tom is Father Kelly's nephew,' Amy said quickly.

'Why are you here?' Jim demanded of Tom.

Tom wasn't sure whether Amy's father meant Tonypandy or the picket line so he gave both explanations. 'To say goodbye to my uncle because I'm on my way to America. There was a spot of bother in town. I offered to escort Miss Watkins here as my uncle was busy on parish business.'

'What kind of bother?' Jim asked Amy.

'One of the London policemen told me to warn Jack that he's been seen digging in the drift mines.'

'Damn him,' Jack said angrily.

'Language, boy. Ladies present,' his father yelled.

'What are we supposed to do, Dad? Freeze and starve to death so Arnold Craggs and the management can make us work for next to nothing again?'

'Quiet, Jack. We'll talk about this when we get home.'

'Mr Kelly, you've met my father Jim Watkins. This is my eldest brother Jack and my brother Mark.' Amy tried to change the subject before Jack started an argument that would put their father in an even worse mood. 'Where's Mathew?'

'Helping the farmer with his potatoes,' Jack answered. It was the excuse the miners gave the police whenever they came looking for someone. It meant that Mathew was doing something he shouldn't. Like searching for wood and coal on colliery property.

Jim finally shook hands with Tom. 'I'm sorry if I misjudged you, boy. A lot of the blacklegs are Irish. However, there isn't a man or woman in Tonypandy who doesn't respect your uncle. He's a good man.'

'Thank you, sir.'

'Go home, Amy,' Jim ordered. 'It's freezing

and likely to get colder. Tell your mother we'll be home around seven o'clock.'

'I will, Dad.'

'Thank Enyd for the tea?' Gwilym held up his tin can.

'I will, Uncle Gwilym.'

'There's no need to walk Amy home,' Jim said to Tom. 'She knows the way.'

'It's me that doesn't know the way, Mr Watkins. I told my uncle I'd meet him back at the soup kitchen. I'll never find it from here without Miss Watkins's help.'

'I have to go there anyway, Dad, to help out.' Amy pulled the hood of her cloak over her bonnet. The temperature seemed to have dropped since she had stopped walking.

'Aren't you meeting the boys to hunt rabbits with the dogs today, Mark?' Jim asked.

'Yes, Dad.'

'Then you can walk Amy and Mr Kelly to the hall.'

Mark pushed his hands deep into the pockets of his threadbare working jacket in an effort to keep warm. 'If we're going, Amy, let's go.'

'Hope you have more luck today than you did yesterday, Mark. I probably won't see you again, Mr Kelly, so good luck in America.' Jim couldn't help smiling at the look of disappointment on Tom's face.

Chapter Three

'I was surprised to see the picket line so quiet. I walked Miss Watkins there because my uncle thought there might be trouble,' Tom said to Mark when they headed towards town. With her father's attitude and with her brother there beside them, Tom hadn't offered Amy his arm.

'Fighting only breaks out when management try to smuggle blacklegs in. Would you believe it, Amy? They hid them in an empty coal cart this morning. Dad and some of the others stopped it from going through the gates. They climbed up and lifted the cover to find six of the bastards.'

'Language.' Tom corrected him.

'They are bastards,' Mark repeated. 'Amy knows they are bastards. Hanging is too good for a blackleg prepared to steal a striker's job by working for less than a living wage. As Dad said, most of them are Irish.'

'You can't blame all the Irish for the actions of a few.' Amy drew her basket beneath her cloak in an effort to warm her hands. 'Father Kelly is Irish and he's the kindest, most unselfish man I know.'

'The problem with us Irish is that we've been starved and beaten by the English for so long, we'll do anything to survive.' Tom spoke quietly, but his comment angered Mark.

'Do you think that being treated badly by the English gives you Irish the right to come here and take our jobs?'

'No. I was only trying to explain why we Irish are so desperate. I've seen the soldiers and police here. It's like home. English officers watch every move we Irish make. The English have only just started on you here, in Wales. Think what you'd feel like if the English had been policing you for hundreds of years.'

'That's why we're fighting them now,' Mark said. 'We won't let the upper classes starve and beat us for hundreds of years.'

'Mark, look, Huw is waving to you from the mountain.' Amy pointed up the hill.

'He's got Nero and Brutus. He must have fetched them from our garden.'

'Our dogs,' Amy explained to Tom. 'Go on, Mark. Don't keep Huw waiting.'

'Dad said I was to walk you to the kitchen.'

'It's more important you try your luck at catching rabbits. It's two weeks since you caught one.'

'You know as well as I do why Dad wanted me to take you home.' Mark glared at Tom.

'I've never known such suspicious people,' Tom complained. 'As there's no one else to speak up for me, I'll have to do it myself. My uncle and brother are priests. I'm a good, God-fearing, clean-living man, who treats ladies with respect. Now tell me, what could I do to your sister in the middle of town other than talk to her and walk her home?'

'I don't know?' Mark said. 'What could you do to her?'

'Huw's still waving, Mark,' Amy said before Tom could answer. When Mark still didn't move, she added, 'If you go now, I won't tell Dad and Mam I saw you kissing Susie James in the back lane last week.'

'You wouldn't dare?'

'Try me,' Amy replied.

'Some sisters are sneaks.'

'And some brothers do what they are told. Go on, Brutus is barking. If you keep Huw waiting much longer, the police will turn up. You know how they hate our dogs.'

'Only the ones we've trained to attack constables. See you back at the house, Sis. Goodbye, Tom. Good luck in America.'

'I know I'm on my way to America, but your family seem keen to get me there as quickly as possible.' Tom offered Amy his arm after Mark ran off.

'It's the strike. It's made us suspicious of everyone.'

'Not me surely?'

'Even sweet talking Irishmen,' she insisted. 'And I have to go home before I go to the soup kitchen. I need to pick up our jug.'

'Don't they have enough jugs in the kitchen?'

'Yes. But I want to get ours filled. Any striker or member of a striker's family can have a free meal in the kitchen. Our family, like most of the others, prefer to pay a shilling to get their jug filled in the kitchen. We like to eat together at home.'

'They don't fill jugs for nothing?' he asked.

'The charities and churches who run the soup kitchens can't afford to. They get some donations of food but not enough to feed everyone.'

'I'm looking forward to meeting your mother. Is she likely to be as wary of me as your father and brothers?' Tom lifted his cap to an old lady who stopped and stared at them.

'It's cold today, isn't it, Mrs Jones?' Amy said to the elderly lady. 'I can't take you home to meet my mother,' she whispered to Tom when they moved on.

'Are you afraid that your mother won't take to me?'

'She's been talking to the other women who work in the kitchen. So, she already thinks there's something going on between us. I only hope the gossips haven't told her that we've been walking together.'

'The gossips won't get to your house before we do.'

'You don't know the gossips in this town.'

'You haven't taken many young men home?' He was asking her for information and she knew it.

'Everyone knows everyone else in Tonypandy. So, the answer to your question is, I haven't taken any strange young men home. I turn left here. You go straight on and take the third left. You can't miss the soup kitchen. Your uncle's house, the church and the church hall will be right in front of you.'

He sighed. 'That means I'll have to do without you for hours.'

She laughed. 'Half an hour at the most.'

'I'll follow you to your house like a stray dog.'

'In which case I'll throw stones at you to make you go away.'

'I'll dodge them.'

Cross now, Amy said, 'You are the most annoying man.'

'Get used to me. I intend to keep on annoying you until you agree to marry me.'

Amy stopped and unhooked her arm from Tom's. 'See you later, Mr Kelly.'

'I'll be lonely walking all that way by myself.'

'The streets are full of people.'

'Too full.' He pulled her into a shop doorway when an angry crowd appeared in Dunraven Street from a side street.

Half a dozen men were pushing a painfully thin man forward ahead of the mob behind them. He was dressed in a thin white shirt open to his waist. His throat, skeletal legs and feet were bare. He was soaking wet and shivering like a dog. His skin was bluish-grey from the cold. When he reached the centre of the road, he tripped over a tram line. He fell and struggled to climb to his feet. The people around him kept him on his knees. They pulled his hair and hit him with their fists and sticks. Women jeered and children pushed in to spit on him.

'Don't.' Amy gripped Tom's arm, holding him back when he stepped forward.

He closed his hand over hers. 'Someone has to help him. The police and soldiers are just standing there, watching.'

'Because they know the mob will turn on them if they interfere.'

'A dog shouldn't be treated like that.'

'A dog shouldn't. But a blackleg should. You're a stranger. You'll be treated the same as him if you take his side.'

'They'll kill him.'

'And possibly you, if you try to help him. Think of your uncle if you won't think of yourself. That man knew what he was doing when he agreed to cross the picket and work for management.'

'No man would risk being shamed the way he is.'

'If his family were starving, he might.' Tears fell from Amy's eyes. She turned her back on Tom and the ugly scene.

The man finally dragged himself upright. Tom watched the mob drive him up the street.

'I have to go home.'

Tom reached for Amy's hand. 'I'll take you and no arguments.'

Amy walked on and Tom quickened his step to keep up with her.

'Where are they taking him?' he asked.

'They'll force him to go over the mountain and wait to make sure he doesn't come back.'

'Without shoes or trousers? He'll catch his death of cold in this rain.'

'Blacklegs have ended up in hospital with broken bones but none have been killed.'

'I knew tempers were running high here,' Tom said. 'But I didn't know how high.'

'Can we talk about something else?' Amy pleaded.

'Like our wedding?'

'Sensible things,' she said seriously.

'What's sensible? My mother taught me never to talk about religion or politics to a lady. That doesn't leave anything else.'

'It leaves everything important: art, poetry, music, books, opera, theatre.'

'You have an opera house here in Tonypandy?'

'We do. And a theatre. Before the strike, opera and theatre companies came up from London to play here. They put on shows three times a day, so all the miners could see them no matter what shift they were working.'

'Travelling theatre companies used to the visit the village I grew up in. They were never from London. But we had one from Dublin once. What's your favourite book?'

'There's so many it's impossible to choose.'

'You read a lot?'

'As much as I can, in between helping my mother run the house. We have a library in the Miner's Institute. I've read all of Dickens' novels. My favourite is *A Tale of Two Cities*.'

'Mine too, although I find it hard to believe that any man would volunteer to be executed.'

'He did it for love.'

'Now that I've met you, I can see that a man would give up his life for love.'

She moved the conversation on quickly. 'I enjoyed reading *Wuthering Heights* and *Jane Eyre*, but I didn't like *Shirley* or *Villette*.'

'What about Walter Scott? And the Irish writers. Have you read *The Picture of Dorian Gray*?'

Tom continued to watch Amy's face while she talked about books. And while he looked and listened, he built an imaginary mansion in America. He filled it with the fine furniture he'd seen in the shop windows in Cork. He added books, pictures, electric lamps, velvet curtains, carpets and a marble bathroom. He pictured himself and Amy there, reading poetry to one another as they sat, side by side on a sofa in front of a roaring fire.

All he had to do was make his fortune. And the mansion and Amy would be his.

Enyd had come back from the soup kitchen and was hard at work, when Amy and Tom walked up the street. She had finished washing her doorstep and the pavement in front of her house, and had brought out fresh water to clean her windows. She dropped the rag she was using into her bucket when she saw Amy.

'Hello, Amy, Mr Kelly.' Enyd nodded to him.

Tom removed his cap in spite of the rain. 'I'm sorry, ma'am. I recognise you from the soup kitchen, but my uncle has introduced me to so many people that I haven't remembered them all.'

'I understand.'

He held out his hand.

Enyd wiped hers in her apron before shaking his. 'Your uncle tells me you're on your way to America.'

'I think the whole of Tonypandy knows that, ma'am.'

Enyd looked at his worn tweed suit and crumpled flannel shirt. 'You've no thoughts of becoming a priest like Father Kelly?'

'No, ma'am.'

She turned Tom's hands over. They were rough and scarred. His nails were broken but they weren't blackened. And there were none of the blue scars that marked the colliers' skins. Amy suspected that her aunt thought Tom was a blackleg.

Tom knew that Enyd was trying to find out what kind of work he'd done. 'I was a farmer in Ireland, ma'am. It was a hard way to try and make a living.'

'Even worse than mining in the Rhondda?'

'About as badly paid. That's why I'm on my way to America.'

'You picked a fine time for your visit.'

Not wanting to talk about what they'd seen in town, Amy interrupted. 'Uncle Gwilym said to say thank you for the tea, Auntie Enyd.'

'You're not Amy's mother?' Tom asked in surprise.

'No, I'm not.' Enyd corrected Tom's mistake. 'But Amy's as dear to me as if she was my own flesh and blood.'

'Would you like me to pick up a jug of soup for you at the kitchen, Auntie?'

'No, thank you, love. I'll be up there myself later on. We got a donation of fifty pounds of cooking apples this morning. The committee will need all the help they can get to peel and stew them.'

'We'll see you there. Bye, Auntie Enyd. Come on, Tom. I live across the road.'

Enyd picked up her bucket. It was time to go in, get her cloak and walk to the soup kitchen. She was looking forward to the warmth of the church hall.

She watched Amy enter her house and hang her cloak on a peg in the hall. Tom was taking his time wiping his feet on the rag rug in the porch.

Mary and Jim Watkins hadn't found any of the local boys, who'd tried to court Amy, good enough for their daughter. So Enyd doubted they'd look kindly on an Irishman. Even one who was Father Kelly's nephew.

That was a pity, given the love she'd seen in Tom Kelly's eyes when he'd looked at Amy. But more especially the love in Amy's bright blue eyes when she'd looked back at Tom.

Chapter Four

'Why did you walk Amy home, Mr Kelly?' Mary Watkins asked after Amy introduced them.

'I asked her to show me the way to the soup kitchen, Mrs Watkins. I told my uncle, Father Kelly, that I'd meet him there later. I'd never have found my own way back to the church hall from the picket line.'

'So, you walked Amy down to the picket as well, Mr Kelly.' Mary didn't hide her annoyance.

'We met by chance, in the main street. My uncle was showing me the town. He got a message asking him to call on one of his parishioners after we set off. If he hadn't been busy, he would have walked with Miss Watkins. A police constable stopped to talk to her. My uncle was concerned that they might do so again. I offered to take his place.'

Mary turned to her daughter. 'Why did a constable stop you, Amy?'

'He was asking questions about Jack.'

'And the drift mines?' Mary frowned.

Amy felt the need to explain to her mother

why she'd brought Tom home. 'Mr Kelly would have walked straight to the soup kitchen from town if I hadn't been upset, Mam. The strikers were white-shirting a blackleg again. It was horrible. He fell and they were hitting him.'

'What's horrible is the way some men are prepared to work for less than a living wage to steal another man's job,' Mary said. 'Remember, Amy, if Arnold Craggs and the blacklegs win this strike, there'll soon be no food on this table.'

'I forgot to ask, Miss Watkins,' Tom said. 'Why did they put a white shirt on the man?'

'So they'll be able to see him in the dark, if he tries to creep back into town at night. The miners want to make sure the blacklegs stay away once they've driven them out of Tonypandy,' Mary informed him. 'Did you recognise the blackleg, Amy?'

'No, Mam.'

'Then he'll be one of the foreigners brought in to steal the miners' jobs. I'm happier knowing he's not a neighbour.'

'Auntie Enyd told me that a load of cooking apples have been donated to the soup kitchen. I need to go up there early to help peel them.' Amy opened the dresser and took out the family's largest enamelled jug.

'I hope you don't mind me walking to the soup kitchen with Miss Watkins, Mrs Watkins.' Tom smiled at Amy's mother. But she refused to be swayed by his charm.

'Looks like I have little choice in the matter. But I'll send one of your brothers up to walk you back, Amy. Wait for him.'

'Yes, Mam.' Amy went into the passage and lifted the cloak from the peg.

'It was nice meeting you, Mrs Watkins.' Tom pulled his cap from his pocket.

Mary Watkins gave him the goodbye he'd been expecting. 'Good luck in America, Mr Kelly.'

'I've had warmer welcomes when there's been frost in the air and ice on the ground.' Tom put his cap on when he and Amy were in the street.

'I told you, everyone in town is on edge.'

'And ready to take their tempers out on me.' Tom shrugged. 'That's all right. My back is broad.'

'I won't take your arm while we can be seen from the street,' she said, when he offered it to her.

'I thought Irish mas and pas were strict with their daughters. Your Welsh mams and dads are ten times worse.'

They left the street and took a mountain path. Tom could just make out the Catholic Church in the distance.

'You can't blame parents for looking after their children,' Amy said.

'No you can't, but I'd look after you as well. Given the chance.' He drew closer to her.

'Please don't start that again.' She changed the subject. 'How are you at peeling apples?'

'I'm better at chopping wood.'

'Then Father Kelly will put you on fuel duty.'

'He's had me on cleaning duties first thing all week. I had to sweep out the hall, before I'd even had breakfast this morning.'

'And he watched you?' Amy knew that Father Kelly never asked anyone to do anything he wouldn't do himself.

'He went out with the rag and bone man on his cart to look for scrap wood to feed the range. They came back with a load of logs.'

'I wonder where they found them.'

'I asked him, and he told me not to ask.'

'The miners working the drifts have offered to supply the kitchen with coal. He won't take it in case the police come in and find it. No one in Tonypandy has any stocks. The only way of getting coal is by breaking the law. Although I can't understand why it's illegal to dig up and take what's sitting there.'

'That's the gentry for you. They use crooked laws to lay claim to everything, even things they don't want. It's their way of keeping the working man down.'

'You talk like my father. Are you a Marxist?'

'I believe in freedom and a man being paid a living wage. But freedom doesn't exist in Ireland. And a living wage is just a dream for most people.'

When they drew close to the church hall, Amy saw a dozen boys playing football with a tin can. Behind them women and children had formed a queue, although the soup kitchen wasn't due to start serving meals for another two hours.

'So many hungry people with nothing to do.' Tom spoke as if he knew what Amy was thinking.

'Unlike them, we have plenty to do if they are going to get their supper.' Amy opened the back door of the hall, pushed down the hood of her cloak and called out, 'Good afternoon, everyone.'

Amy only noticed the silence after she'd hung her cloak on a peg. She turned around. Two constables and Sergeant Martin were with

Father Kelly. At a nod from Sergeant Martin the constables stepped forward and held Tom's arms.

'What are you doing?' Amy asked.

'Not that it's any of your business, Miss Watkins, but this man is coming with us,' a constable replied.

'You can't arrest him. He hasn't done anything,' she protested.

'We're not arresting Mr Kelly, Miss Watkins,' Sergeant Martin informed her.

One of the constables holding Tom pushed his helmet back, away from his face. Amy recognised Constable Shipton.

'We're here to remind Mr Kelly of his responsibilities, Miss Watkins.'

'What responsibilities?' Amy looked to Tom, but he said nothing.

'We'll discuss this in private.' Father Kelly led the way. The sergeant and constables followed with Tom.

Amy watched them leave the hall. Then she joined Enyd and the other ladies. They had stopped work when she and Tom had arrived. 'Why are the police taking Tom Kelly, Auntie Enyd?'

'I've no idea, love. The officers walked in ten minutes ago asking for Father Kelly's nephew. When he told them that he wasn't here, they said they'd wait. That's all I know. Come on, ladies,' Enyd commanded briskly. 'Start working. We've a queue of hungry people waiting out in the rain.'

The women turned back to the tables and carried on preparing vegetables and scraping the last scraps of mutton from bones.

'What do you want to do, Amy? Peel apples, or clean vegetables?' Betty Morgan, a strike leader's wife, handed her a knife.

'She'll do the apples with me, Betty.' Enyd made room for Amy to join her.

Betty went to the cupboard and opened the door. 'There's enough flour and sugar to make a couple of tarts. If we have apple left over, we'll serve it stewed with the last of tins of condensed milk.'

'Soup and afters,' Enyd declared. 'Our customers will think it's Christmas.'

The women laughed. Amy took her apron from her basket and tied it over her dress. She picked up an apple and started peeling, but her thoughts were with Tom Kelly. She couldn't stop wondering why the police had come to "fetch him".

'I signed up to work in the Glamorgan Colliery

when I was back in Ireland. But no one said anything to me about a strike, Sergeant Martin.' Tom remained calm and polite for his uncle's sake.

'Did you sign a legal document agreeing to work in the colliery for as long as your labour was needed?' Sergeant Martin asked.

'Yes, but no one said anything about the workers in the colliery striking,' Tom repeated.

'As payment for signing the document you were given a ship's ticket from Ireland to Wales?' Sergeant Martin asked.

'I was,' Tom agreed.

'If you refuse to honour the contract, Mr Craggs has the right to demand repayment of your passage money. Plus £50 compensation so that he can hire someone to take your place.'

'Instead of upholding the law, Sergeant Martin, you and the constables are working for Mr Craggs and colliery management now,' Father Kelly said.

'We're enforcing the law, Father,' Sergeant Martin replied. 'Your nephew has admitted that he entered a legal contract. Now it appears he wants to break it.'

'I can't pay anyone fifty farthings, let alone pounds.' Tom's voice rose sharply. 'No working man has that kind of money and you know it. My passage from Ireland was three pounds.'

'And your train ticket to Tonypandy from Cardiff docks another pound.' Constable Shipton took a piece of paper from his pocket and read it. 'Mr Craggs wants you and your labour, or fifty-four pounds in compensation. He wants it now.'

'If my nephew can't pay what he owes, Mr Craggs can send round the bailiffs.' Father Kelly sat down behind his desk. Like Tom, he was finding it hard to control his temper.

'If Mr Kelly has fifty-four pounds in goods, we'll take them. If you want to pay his debt for him, Father, we'll collect the money,' the sergeant said.

'You heard my nephew. He hasn't fifty farthings. All I own are my clothes. Everything you see in this house belongs to the church.'

'Then there would be no point in Mr Craggs hiring bailiffs.'

'None,' Tom agreed.

'Even if he did, you'd be long gone by the time they arrived here,' Constable Shipton eyed Tom.

Tom didn't deny it. 'I saw what's happening in Tonypandy this morning. I'm no blackleg and I'll not take another man's job.'

'That's your last word on the subject?' Constable Shipton asked.

'I'll deal with this, Constable.' Sergeant Martin looked at Tom.

'I've said all I'm going to.' Tom folded his arms across his chest.

'You leave me no choice but to arrest you for fraud.' The Sergeant didn't look happy at the prospect.

'Go ahead, arrest me,' Tom said.

'You slept in this house last night?' Sergeant Martin asked.

'As I have done for almost a week,' Tom told him.

'Then we will also have to arrest your uncle for harbouring a criminal, and his housekeeper for feeding you.'

'You can't do that, Sergeant,' Tom protested.

'We can and we will,' Sergeant Martin said firmly.

'The colliers have been creating trouble in the valley for months. There's a backlog of cases waiting to go before the courts.' Constable Shipton taunted Tom. 'You, your uncle and his housekeeper could be kept in prison on remand for months.'

'My uncle and his housekeeper aren't to blame for my actions,' Tom insisted.

'They aided and abetted you,' Shipton pointed out.

'They're needed to run the soup kitchen,' Tom said.

'We're needed to bring in donations and distribute what little food there is,' Father Kelly pleaded. 'Without us, people will go hungry.'

'The hungrier the better in my opinion.' Constable Shipton narrowed his eyes. 'If the people around here were really starving, the men would return to work. Then the constables and soldiers from outside Wales could go home to their families.'

'That's enough, Shipton.' Sergeant Martin faced Tom. 'I'll give you a choice, boy. Come with us quietly and do the work that you promised to do, and we'll let your uncle and his housekeeper go free.'

'I'll come with you.'

Tom saw Constable Shipton reach for the handcuffs clipped to his belt. He held out his hands.

'If you give us your word that you'll come quietly, we won't handcuff you,' Sergeant Martin offered.

'I'll come quietly.'

'Put your handcuffs away, Shipton.'

'Where are you taking Tom?' Father Kelly asked.

'Eventually to the colliery. Mr Craggs has had beds made up for the workers in the lamp room.'

'I'm sorry, Uncle.' Tom apologised. 'If I'd known what it was like in Tonypandy, I would never have come here and shamed you.'

'Why didn't you tell me that you'd signed a contract with management when you arrived?'

'Because I thought I was just taking a job that paid my passage here. It's a long way to America. I didn't even have the fare out of Ireland. They told me that, if I worked here for a few months, I'd earn enough to buy a ship's ticket to New York.'

'You must have heard of the strike we have here, even in Ireland.'

'I'd heard of it, but I didn't realise how much the miners were suffering because of it. I only found out when I saw it for myself. The last thing I'd do is knowingly hurt you, Uncle. You have to believe me.'

'I believe you, boy,' Father Kelly murmured.

'Tell the strike leaders the truth. That I [illegible]n't tell you about the contract I signed with [illegible]anagement. If it helps, disown me.

Please tell Miss Watkins that I would never steal another man's job. Not willingly.'

'I'll tell her boy. And I'll tell the strike leaders that you didn't know what you were doing when you signed the agent's paper. Not that it will do any good. Tempers are running too high for anyone to want to listen to the truth.'

Father Kelly watched Constable Shipton march Tom out of the door.

Chapter Five

Amy tried to concentrate on peeling apples. She kept glancing at the door, watching and waiting for Father Kelly or Tom to return. She started every time it opened, and tried not to show her disappointment when it wasn't either of them. She heard Father Kelly talking to someone before he finally entered the hall. Seconds later she heard the thunder of metal-heeled boots ringing on stone. When she looked out of the window she saw a small boy running down the hill.

'Father Kelly?' A dozen women left their tables and ran up to him.

The priest stepped back towards the door. 'Please, ladies, don't ask me any questions. Just get the supper ready for those who need it. If anyone wants me urgently, I'll be in the house.'

For the first time since Amy had started helping in the soup kitchen, everyone worked in silence. Before they opened the doors to the queue outside, Betty Morgan filled her jug for her.

Betty also gave her a plate wrapped in brown paper. 'Apple tart. Push it in the bottom of your basket, before anyone sees it,' she whispered.

Amy shook her head. Her father insisted that, for the duration of the strike, they had to share what little they had. He believed, if anyone took extra food for their own family, it would lead to trouble. The miners needed to work together, not fight one another.

'My father wouldn't let me take it, Mrs Morgan.'

'Before you say another word, I saw the twins walking to school this morning. They need more nourishment. Your mother will see they get the largest slices.'

Amy took the plate. She tucked the tart beneath the cloth she used to cover the jug. Setting her basket aside, she took her place beside Enyd at the serving table. Betty Morgan opened the doors and people moved into the hall. The adults pushed the children to the front so they would be served first.

Although they were busy, time had never moved so slowly for Amy. She felt as though she had been ladling soup into bowls for days when her brother Mathew appeared. He removed his cap, nodded to the ladies who were in the hall and joined her behind the table.

'If you've come to walk me home, you're early,' Amy said.

Enyd pointed to the sink. 'Some jobs can be done as well by a man as a woman. There are dishes that need washing, Mathew.'

'I walked up with my father, and Ned Morgan, the Evanses and the other strike leaders,' Mathew told them. 'Father Kelly called a meeting. They're holding it in his house.'

Amy's mouth went dry and her heart started pounding so fast she felt faint. 'The police came here earlier and took Tom Kelly away.'

'Tom Kelly's a blackleg.' Mathew didn't bother to lower his voice. 'And you've been seen all over town with him, Amy. Dad told me to take you home. He wants to talk to you when he gets back from the meeting.'

Amy didn't argue but she refused to believe what Mathew had told her. She untied her apron, folded it into her basket, lifted down her cloak and slipped it over her shoulders.

'You are never to see Tom Kelly or talk to him again, Amy. Is that clear?' Jim Watkins's voice rang loudly. It echoed against the stone walls and the cold flagstone floor as he faced his daughter across their kitchen.

'Are you sure Tom's a blackleg, Dad?'

Jim softened his tone when he saw the pain in Amy's eyes. 'Father Kelly had it from Tom himself.'

'I don't believe it.'

'Father Kelly didn't want to believe it either, love, but it's true.'

'Where is Tom now?' she asked.

'We don't know. Sergeant Martin's hidden him and the other blacklegs. Arnold Craggs has sorted beds in the colliery for the blacklegs they've hired to do what they call essential work. Although what essential work, no one knows. Mr Craggs refused the union's offer to allow skilled men in to man the pumps to stop the pits from flooding.'

'Is Tom in the pit now?'

'I don't think so. We stopped every cart that went in through the gates today. Management tried to bring men in. As far as I know they failed every time. It can only be a matter of time before they try again.'

'What will happen to Tom if you and the other miners catch him?'

'It's not "if", it's "when". You know the answer to that as well as I do. Your mother said you'd seen the white-shirting in town today. It's what all blacklegs have coming to them.'

'Do you have to treat blacklegs like that, Dad?' she pleaded. 'They must be desperate and starving to work for management.' She stopped speaking when she saw the expression on her father's face harden.

'Never question me about union work or judgements, girl?'

'Tom told me about Ireland, Dad. The way he talked about the workers struggling for freedom and a living wage there was just like the way you and the other strike leaders talk here.'

'You don't need to tell me he can talk. Like all Irishmen, he can do that all right. Especially to a young, innocent girl. I saw the way he looked at you. And the way you were looking at and listening to him. But you'll see him and talk to him no more. Is that understood?'

'Yes, Dad.'

'Go to bed.'

Amy took a stub of candle from the box on the mantelpiece and a newspaper spill the twins had made. She pushed the spill into the embers of the fire. Her mother had raked out the coals that were worth saving for their next fire, as soon as their soup had warmed.

She lit the candle, dropped wax on to an old chipped saucer and glued the candle to it with the melted wax.

'The right man will turn up for you one day, Amy,' her father said gruffly.

She knew her father was trying to apologise for being sharp with her. 'No man will be asking any girl to marry him while he's on strike, Dad.'

'I know it feels like it after a year, but this strike won't last for ever.'

'I know it won't, Dad. Good night.' She kissed his cheek, which was rough with stubble. She left the kitchen and went into the hall. Her mother was hanging up the cloak they shared.

'I called on Enyd. She's just come back from the soup kitchen after helping Father Kelly and his housekeeper to clean up.'

'How is Father Kelly?' Amy asked in concern.

'How do you think? Enyd said he's shattered. Who would have thought that his nephew could come here as a blackleg? That's why he sent for the strike leaders. He wanted to explain to them himself. You've spoken to your father?'

'Yes.'

'He told you that you're not to talk to Tom Kelly again? Not that you're likely to see him.'

'He told me.'

'Then up to bed with you.' Mary kissed Amy's cheek. 'Check the twins for me on your way please, love.'

Amy walked up the stairs. She passed her parents' back bedroom door and turned along the landing to the front bedroom her brothers shared. A double and single bed had been crammed in, end to end. There might have been room to walk around them if a wardrobe and chest of drawers hadn't been pushed in as well. The twins were fast asleep, sprawled side by side in the single bed, their arms flung wide out of the sheets and blankets.

Amy kneeled on the bed and tucked their cold arms beneath the bedclothes. She glanced across at the empty double bed her three older brothers shared, before closing the door. They wouldn't be back until after midnight. The younger fitter men took the night shifts on the picket line, because management often tried to smuggle blacklegs in under cover of darkness.

She opened the door to her tiny box room that overlooked the street. The door hit her narrow iron bedstead. At the foot of the bed there was just enough room for her iron-framed washstand. It held a jug, bowl, slop bucket and soap dish. A towel rail was bolted on the side.

Her Sunday dress and her spare skirt and blouse were on hooks behind the door. She kept her underclothes and stockings in an old suitcase under the bed. On the wall behind the door was a black spotted mirror. It had hung in the parlour until her mother had saved enough money to replace it. Above her bed was a framed piece of embroidery, called a sampler.Her grandmother had made it to show her skill at needlework before she'd married.

She set the candle down on the windowsill. Beside it was a toffee tin. It had been a Christmas present when she was five years old. She used it as a jewellery box.

She opened it and lifted out her grandmother's wedding and engagement rings. The simple gold band was worn and scratched. The engagement ring, with its small but real diamond, sparkled in the light of the candle. She remembered the stories her grandmother used to tell her and her brothers about her grandfather.

"Simon came from England, and was sent to my father's house to look for lodgings. He knocked on

the door. Everyone in the Rhondda knows you knock once and walk in. But he was English. He knocked a second time and stood on the step waiting. I opened the door, looked into his eyes and fell in love there and then. We were married six weeks later. Simon bought me the wedding ring with his savings. We set up home in my mother's front parlour. We lived on what was left after he paid my mother rent. The diamond ring came later when your father was born. Simon was so proud of his baby son."

Could it happen that way? Could a girl look at a man and fall in love that quickly? She pictured Tom Kelly, tall, dark and handsome. She remembered the gleam in his eyes when he had looked at her the first time they had met in the soup kitchen. She knew that it could happen that way, because it had happened to her.

Restless, unable to think of anything except Tom, Amy couldn't sleep. She tossed and turned on her bed, wondering where Tom was and what he was doing.

Later she heard her mother and father walk up the stairs. She listened to the soft murmur of their voices as they undressed. Their bedsprings creaked when they climbed into bed. She was still wide awake after the town clock struck midnight. It chimed one o'clock before her brothers came home from the picket.

Jack's whispered "shushes" echoed up the stairs. They were hopeless. They made more noise when they were trying to be quiet than they did during the day. Mathew's voice echoed down the passage from the kitchen. She heard Mark talking to the dogs in their run outside. The door slammed when he visited the "Ty Bach", the little house in the garden that held the toilet.

Her brothers at last climbed the stairs. Their boots thudded on the bare floorboards after they'd unlaced and dropped them. Their shirts and trousers swished when they threw them on to the chest of drawers. Given their muffled laughter and the racket they were making, it was amazing the twins didn't wake.

All three were snoring when she pulled open her curtains and looked through the window. The moon shone down through its halo of mist from a star-filled sky. Something rattled against the glass. She looked down. Unable to believe what she was seeing, she rubbed her eyes.

Below her window, with his palm full of small stones was Tom Kelly.

Chapter Six

Amy stared at Tom in disbelief. She didn't move until he pointed to the front door. She shook her head and pointed to herself and then the pavement. He nodded to show he'd understood. She pulled the curtain across her window and dived out of bed. She lifted her clothes from the iron footboard and began to dress. The more she hurried, the more her fingers fumbled with hooks and buttons.

She pulled her bust shaper on inside-out and decided there wasn't time to turn it. She buttoned her blouse, only to find she'd muddled the buttons and had to begin again. She even managed to put two legs in one leg of her drawers. She rolled on her stockings, fastened them with her garters, tied on her petticoats, slipped on her skirt and picked up her boots. She turned the doorknob, eased the door open and held her breath.

Her three older brothers were still snoring. She took a deep, silent breath and tiptoed past their door and along the landing. She was careful to avoid the floorboard that creaked. She didn't breathe again until she reached the top of the stairs. Her father coughed and she froze. She waited what seemed like hours until silence filled the house once more. Gripping the banister, she crept down the stairs to the front door and reached for the cloak.

Holding the doorknob in her hand because it was likely to rattle, she opened the door. She stepped into the porch and closed the passage door behind her before opening the door to the street.

Tom was standing, pressed against the house wall in a pool of moonlight. She caught hold of his hand. It was ice cold.

She laid her finger over his lips and pointed towards the mountain end of the street. Stopping only to lace on her boots, she ran ahead of him. The air was clear, frosty, the temperature freezing, the moon bright enough to light their way. She headed for the ruins of an old farm cottage. Every bit of wood in the place had been taken by the strikers for fuel. Although the building had no roof, windows or doors, its walls were standing. Once she was inside them, she drew back from the doorway into a dark corner out of sight of any passer-by.

'Are you mad?' she whispered when Tom followed her. 'I know it's the middle of the night but there are people everywhere. The men work the drift mines at this hour. The soldiers and police patrol try to catch them. And management usually move their blacklegs at night.'

'I had to see you,' he murmured. 'I wanted to tell you that, if I had known what it was like here, I would never have signed a contract. The first time my uncle took me out I saw the soldiers and police. I realised then that the struggle here was no different from the one in Ireland. But I'd been tricked into joining the wrong side. When I saw your father and the others on the picket line today, saw what they were going through to fight for a decent wage, I decided I had no choice but to break my contract.'

'You left the soup kitchen with the police.'

'They said they'd arrest my uncle and his housekeeper for helping a criminal if I didn't go with them. That is why I have to go back to the other blacklegs now. I've been a fool and made a terrible mistake. The last thing I can do is let them put my uncle and his housekeeper in prison because of my stupidity.'

'Did the police allow you out to come looking for me?'

'No.' He moved closer to her in the darkness. She saw his breath clouding in the moonlight that streamed through the door. She felt the warmth of his body as he stood almost, but not quite, touching her. 'They put a dozen of us in the hayloft above stables at the back of a pub. They told us to wait there until they can move us into the colliery.'

'What pub?'

'One of the men with us said it was the White Hart. He recognised the yard. I didn't see any more of the place, because they took us in under thick sheets in a butcher's cart. Two policemen were left to guard us. But they locked the stable door and disappeared. After a couple of hours I decided it was worth trying to find you to explain why I signed the contract. I stuffed my jacket with straw and pushed it under one of the blankets they gave us. The other men promised to cover for me if the officers came back. It's not likely they'll have to. When I climbed out of the skylight on to the roof, I saw the policemen in the pub kitchen. They were stretched out in chairs in front of a fire with their eyes closed.'

It was only then Amy noticed that Tom was

in shirt sleeves. 'You must be freezing without your jacket.'

'I'm used to the cold.'

'Do you have to go back to the stable?' she pleaded.

'You know I do. I've brought enough disgrace on my uncle as it is. Besides, the other blacklegs aren't a bad lot. Just desperate hungry men.'

'Work for management and you'll be white-shirted like that poor man today.'

'I know.'

'I can't bear to think of that happening to you, Tom.' She looked up at him. He was a shadow in the darkness. She couldn't read the expression on his face.

'Everything I told you about Ma dying and having nothing to keep me in Ireland was true. The landlord didn't want me staying on in Ma's cottage. The rent is a quarter of what the farm produces in a year. He'll get more out of a young family than a single man. I told my sisters to share out Ma and Pa's few sticks of furniture, not that any of them were worth much. All I was left with was the clothes on my back. After I paid for Ma's funeral, I didn't have a penny to my name. As it was, I had to sleep under my eldest sister's table for a week while I worked off the cost of Ma's funeral by digging the priest's garden.'

'Was that when you signed the contract with the colliery management?'

'That came later, after I walked to Cork. I hoped to find work there but there was nothing going. Men were fighting one another for an hour's work unloading ships on the docks. That's when someone told me there was an agent from Wales, signing up men for the coal mines. I'd heard a bit about what it was like here, because my uncle had written to Ma and Pa over the years. He said the mine was terrible underground. But I thought it was too good an opportunity to miss when the agent offered to pay for my travel. He promised I'd get two pounds a week while I worked in the pit.'

'They promised you two pounds a week?' Amy was stunned. At the best of times her father had only brought home one pound ten shillings. And he was a highly skilled man.

'They said they'd have to take a pound a week from my wages for my keep and to pay back the cost of travelling here. Even so, I thought that if I worked here for a year I'd save enough to buy my ticket to America. And have money in my pocket when I got there.'

Amy grabbed his arm when she heard footsteps. They moved further back against the wall. The footsteps drew nearer and nearer. Amy's heart was pounding so loudly that she was sure whoever it was would hear it.

The footsteps passed and she wilted with relief. Tom wrapped his arms around her.

'I'm so sorry. I love you and all I've brought you is trouble.'

She lifted her face to his. He brushed his lips over hers, so gently and lightly, she couldn't be sure he'd kissed her. She drew even closer to him and locked her hands around his neck. He pressed his lips down harder. The cold, the night, the fear of being seen, even thoughts of the future faded. She could think of nothing except Tom and his kisses.

New and wonderful feelings flooded through her body. Nothing had made her feel as alive as Tom's caresses. Her entire life had been building up to this one moment. Now it had arrived, it was perfect. She and Tom belonged together. Nothing – not even colliery management and the strikers – could change that.

Tom went to the ruined doorway and looked out. 'There's no one about. I'll walk you back.'

'When will I see you again?'

'If I can get away I'll come to your window tomorrow night. I'll throw up a stone as I did tonight.'

'How did you know it was my window and not my brothers'?'

'Because the window over the front door always belongs to the smallest room. I didn't think your Pa would make five boys sleep there.'

'You took a risk.'

'You're here, with me. It was worth it.'

'Tom, what are we going to do?' she asked. She remembered her father's stern warning not to see Tom again.

'I don't know,' he replied honestly. 'I need to think, and I can't do that when I'm with you. We'd better go. Don't say a word on the way.' He stole a last kiss from her and guided her outside.

Enyd Jenkins couldn't sleep for thinking about Father Kelly. She had never seen him as upset as he had been when she'd helped clean the kitchen that evening. She had tried to explain the issue to Gwilym when he had come home from the picket line. Gwilym had seen it from a strikers' point of view.

"A blackleg is a blackleg, Enyd, whether or not he's been tricked into signing a contract with management. Tom Kelly might be Father Kelly's nephew, but he's no different from any other black-hearted Irishman. They come to Wales to steal our jobs. If we get hold of him, we'll beat him seven shades of black and blue and white-shirt him out of town. Father Kelly will have to live with it as best he can. I agree with you, Father Kelly is a good man. But his nephew is less than dirt as far as I and every right-thinking union man is concerned."

After making that judgement Gwilym had gone to bed. Enyd had followed him upstairs but, unable to sleep, had gone back downstairs an hour later. The parlour was no colder than the kitchen so she had gone in there. Because she and Gwilym had no children to feed, they were surviving the strike better than most families. She hadn't had to pawn the china she had inherited from her mother. Or sell the books she and Gwilym had collected. She still had her one piece of valuable jewellery. It was a piece she never wore, and she had been careful to keep it hidden from Gwilym. She unlocked the drawer in the bookcase that had belonged to Gwilym's father and reached into the back.

Her hand closed around a small red leather case. She took it out and opened it. Lying on a bed of blue velvet was a gold locket. She sprang the catch at the side and looked at the two photographs it contained. She was still staring at them ten minutes later when she heard a noise outside.

She read the parlour clock. Half past three. Were the soldiers or police out trying to catch the miners working the drifts?

She blew out the candle, went to the window and pushed the lace aside. Amy Watkins was standing outside her front door. Next to her was Tom Kelly. He had his back to her, but Enyd was sure it was him. There weren't many men in Tonypandy as tall as Tom. As she watched, Tom bent his head to Amy's, cupped her face in his hands, and kissed her.

Enyd felt as though her heart had stopped. Fearful, terrified for Amy, she wanted to take her away. She would have, if she could have thought of somewhere where Amy would be safe.

Chapter Seven

Tom walked in the shadows of the houses when he left Amy's house. He crept back down the hill towards the town and the White Hart. The sound of voices raised in anger echoed from the main street. He looked around the corner and dived into a shop doorway. Hundreds of strikers filled the street. Some of the men were holding their arms above their heads, tossing white-shirted men in the air.

Tom saw one man slip down between the strikers. There was a scream when the man hit the road. The strikers hid his body from view. Tom looked at the faces of the men who were being thrown high by the crowd. He recognised the blacklegs who had been locked into the stable loft with him. Hoping no one would see him, he crouched low.

The blacklegs' arms and legs were bound by rope. Across the road a striker had climbed a lamp post. Hooking his arm around the crossbar for support, the man wound a rope around the lamp. Half a dozen other strikers handed up a blackleg. The miner clinging to the post tied the rope around the blackleg's chest, and hooked it beneath his armpits. The miner pulled the rope tight and knotted it before letting the prisoner go. The blackleg swung free, his bare legs and feet flailing in the freezing air.

Tom looked down the street and saw five other blacklegs strung up to lamp posts in the same way. Each had attracted a crowd. They dangled helplessly in mid-air as men and women took turns to beat them with carpet beaters and sticks.

The striker who had tied the last blackleg jumped down and moved on to the next lamp. Tom looked for the constables who were supposed to be guarding them. They were nowhere to be seen. A dozen police officers had gathered at the other end of the street, close to the police station. They were watching the strikers. Not one of them had unhooked the truncheons they wore on their belts. Tom didn't blame them. A dozen men could do nothing against hundreds. He only hoped his fellow blacklegs were fit enough to cope with the rough treatment they were getting.

He looked back up the hill. The street was empty and quiet. He didn't dare risk entering the main street or returning to the stables. Too many people had seen him around town with Amy and his uncle. A man of his height was easily recognised. Neither could he return to Amy's house. If her father and brothers should find him, they'd probably beat him. Not only for being a blackleg, but for daring to talk to Amy. Besides, he didn't want to put her or her family at risk. That left only the ruined cottage.

Could he reach it without anyone seeing him?

'What's the matter with you this morning, Enyd?' Gwilym Jenkins asked. 'You're behaving as though you can't wait to get me out of the house. I might want a second cup of tea.'

'Then you can drink what's left in the pot. I'd like to go to the soup kitchen early for once.' Enyd carried on picking coals from the fire and smothering them with the coal shovel. To her husband's disgust she had begun raking out the fire as soon as he had sat down to breakfast.

'Is something happening in the soup kitchen that I should know about?' Gwilym asked.

'Not that I know of. Father Kelly was very

upset last night. I want to make sure he's all right.'

'You think more of Father Kelly than you do of me,' Gwilym grumbled.

'I do not. You're being silly,' Enyd snapped.

'Am I? Look at yourself? You should be sitting at the table drinking your tea, not playing in the fireplace.'

'I'm not "playing". I'm only trying to save every ounce of coal.'

'For Father Kelly's soup kitchen?'

'You know he burns wood, not coal, in the church hall range, Gwilym.' Enyd sat back on her heels and looked at her husband. 'We're both under enough strain as it is with the strike. Let's not quarrel.'

'I'm not quarrelling with you. I just wish that you'd stick to being a wife.'

'What's that supposed to mean?' In spite of what she'd just said about not quarrelling, Enyd felt anger burning inside her.

'It means I don't want to hear another word from you about Father Kelly or his nephew.'

'Father Kelly has supported every miner during this strike, Gwilym. He's fed the children. He's arranged as many meals as he can for the miners' families and driven miles to gather money and food for the soup kitchens.'

'He invited his black-eyed devil of an Irish nephew to stay under his roof,' Gwilym raged. 'He welcomed him into his home. He even had the cheek to introduce him to Amy Watkins, although the man only came to Tonypandy to take our jobs.'

'Father Kelly didn't know Tom Kelly had signed up to be a blackleg when he arrived. He only found out yesterday.'

'So Father Kelly says.'

'I believe him.'

'I'll not argue any more with you about this, Enyd. I have to be on the picket in half an hour.' Gwilym left the table, went into the hall and lifted his overcoat and cap from a peg.

'Gwilym, don't go like this,' she pleaded.

Gwilym turned back. 'How would you like me to go, Enyd?'

When she didn't answer him, he left the house, slamming the door behind him.

Enyd dropped the tongs and stared at the dying embers of the fire. She didn't know what she should do. She only knew that she had to do something. The question she kept asking herself was what.

Mathew and Mark Watkins drank their tea and ate thin slices of apple tart the next morning before leaving their house for the picket line. Ten minutes later they were back in the house, talking to their father and their brother Jack who were still at the kitchen table.

'You should have seen the blacklegs before the constables cut them down.' Mark moved close to the range. Mary had raked it out but the metal surfaces were still warm. 'They were blue with cold and so stiff the constables had to carry them into the back of their van.'

'Where had management hidden the scum?' Jim asked.

'In the stables behind the White Hart. Ned Morgan told me he had a tip-off they were there.'

'Who told him?' Jack took his boots from beside the range and began to lace them on.

'Ned wouldn't say. But the barmaids and stable boys in the Hart are the daughters and sons of colliers. Any one of them could have said something to the strike committee.' Mathew rubbed his hands together. His fingers were white, wrinkled and numb with cold. 'The police didn't dare go near the blacklegs because so many strikers turned out in the early hours to white-shirt them. They left them hanging from the lamp posts for hours.'

'The strikers hung blacklegs.' Amy clutched

the doorpost for support. She had been outside looking for eggs in the hen house and had only heard the last part of the conversation.

'Not by the neck,' her father said gruffly, 'although they deserved it.'

Amy sank down on the nearest chair.

Mark grinned. 'The colliers hung them from ropes tied around their chests and gave them a good beating. I wish the boys who'd organised it had come here and woken us, so we could have seen it.'

'The men who hung and beat them are barbarians,' Amy said angrily.

'It's barbaric to want to keep your job, is it?' her father asked her.

'No, it isn't. But it's barbaric to beat helpless men.'

'Was Tom Kelly one of the blacklegs?' Jim Watkins asked Mark the question, but he was watching Amy.

'No. He wasn't in the Hart with the others, so management must have hidden him somewhere else. I asked Ned Morgan if he'd seen Tom, but Ned hadn't. They hung eleven blacklegs in all, and the police cut six down before Mathew and I got there. We ran back here because we thought you and Jack would want to know about it. As Gwilym Jenkins and Ned Morgan said, this sends a clear message to management. Don't bring any more blacklegs into Tonypandy.'

'Management isn't in the mood to listen to any messages from the strike committee.' Jim went into the hall and fetched his cap, muffler and coat. He turned to Amy. 'What I said to you yesterday still stands, Amy. If you see Tom Kelly, you are to walk away from him. You are not to look at or talk to him. Understand?'

'I understand,' Amy repeated. She crossed her fingers under cover of her skirt. It was an old saying. Cross your fingers and you can tell a lie. But it wasn't exactly a lie. All she had told her father was that she understood him. She hadn't promised to obey him.

When Enyd Jenkins finished her morning chores, she washed her hands and face in cold water and rolled down her sleeves. She put on her cloak and bonnet, picked up her basket, and crossed the road to the Watkins' house. She knocked on the door once, turned the key and walked down the passage. She stopped to talk to the twins who were on their way to school. Amy was in the kitchen with her mother.

'You're off to the soup kitchen early, Enyd,' Mary said.

'I was hoping Amy would help me pick up a dozen loaves from the baker's on the way. The baker's boy doesn't deliver to the hall before twelve. Father Kelly asked me to make sure we have enough bread in for the babies' breakfasts.'

'You two be careful if you're walking into town,' Mary warned.

'Why?' Enyd asked.

Amy told her what her brothers had said about the blacklegs being hung.

'If the police have cut them down and taken them away, the town will be quiet,' Enyd said. 'It's not too early for you to be going to the soup kitchen is it, Amy?'

'No.'

'Go on admit it,' Mary smiled. 'You two can't wait to get in the warm of the church hall.'

'You're welcome to join us, Mary,' Enyd offered. 'Father Kelly can do with all the help he can get.'

'I'm helping in the school soup kitchen today, so I'll be as warm as you. And don't talk to me about Father Kelly or that nephew of his. Not after the way Tom Kelly walked around town yesterday with this stupid daughter of mine.'

'No one knew he was a blackleg then, Mary. Come on, Amy, let's see if we can get the pick of the loaves when they come out of the oven. The children like them brown and crusty.'

Enyd and Amy walked down the hill in silence. A number of police were in Dunraven Street. They were cutting down the last of the ropes tied around the lamp posts. There was no sign of the blacklegs or the strikers.

'The men have returned to the picket line,' Enyd said.

'It looks like it,' Amy agreed.

'Do you know where Tom Kelly is?' Enyd asked.

'No,' Amy replied. 'What makes you think that I do?'

'Because I saw the two of you outside your front door last night. He was kissing you and you were kissing him right back.'

Amy eyes grew large and frightened. 'You won't tell Mam and Dad, will you, Auntie Enyd? Not for my sake, but for Tom's. You heard what they did to the other blacklegs?'

'Amy, child,' Enyd stared into Amy's eyes. 'Do you know what you're doing?'

'I love him with all my heart and soul, Auntie Enyd.'

'You've known him a week.'

'That was all the time I needed to fall in love with him.'

'Then God help the pair of you.' Enyd shook her head in despair. 'There's nothing more to be said. Are you sure you don't know where he is?'

A tear fell from Amy's eye. She brushed it away. 'I only wish I did.'

Chapter Eight

Enyd and Amy reached the church hall to find a cart parked outside. It was stacked high with sacks of vegetables. Father Kelly was standing next to it talking to the carter.

'Look what Mr Robinson has brought us from the farmers in the Vale of Glamorgan, ladies.' He went to the back of the cart. 'Enough carrots, turnips, potatoes and swedes to keep the kitchen going for a week. Would you be kind enough to show the boys where to take the sacks, Mrs Jenkins?'

'Follow me.' Enyd went to the back door of the hall and held it open so the carter's boys could carry the sacks inside.

Father Kelly shook the carter's hand. 'You and your boys will have a cup of tea with us, won't you, Mr Robinson?'

'We will, thank you, Father. It's been slow, cold, wet work driving here.' The carter climbed down from his cart.

'Mrs Jenkins will find you a table near to the stove so you can have a warm. Amy?'

Father Kelly stopped her as she was about to walk through the door. He took her to one side. 'Sergeant Martin was here before I opened the hall this morning. He told me that Tom went to the police station at first light.'

'He's all right. He's really all right!' Amy cried in relief.

'Sergeant Martin said there's not a mark or a bruise on him. He hid when the strikers broke into the barn last night and took the other blacklegs. You heard what happened to them?'

'I did.' Amy leaned against the wall for support.

'Sergeant Martin said that Tom saw the strikers hanging and beating the others. But the most important thing is he's safe and unhurt.'

'Thank you for telling me, Father Kelly.'

'I'm sorry I introduced you two, Amy. Given that Tom is a blackleg, I've brought you nothing but trouble. Your father must be angry with me.'

'My father's not angry with you, Father Kelly. But he is angry that I was seen around town with Tom.' Amy remembered the kisses Tom had given her. She could still feel his lips on hers. And that made her feel like a traitor to her family and more especially to her father and all the other colliers.

Father Kelly saw that she was upset and changed the subject. 'We have a lot of vegetables to clean today. Thank you for helping.'

'I'm glad of something to do. There's been less housework in our house since the strike started and we haven't had coal. It's amazing how much dust a fire makes.'

'That's what I like. A young girl who can see good in the worst of things.'

'You'll let me know, Father?' Amy didn't have to explain about what.

'If I find out anything more about young Tom? Of course I will, Amy. You like him, don't you?'

'Yes I do. He's funny and he talks like no one else I know, except perhaps you.'

Father Kelly walked to the back of the cart to see how the boys were getting on with unloading.

He thought about what Amy had said, and doubted that it was just Tom's talk that she liked. He had never seen two people fall in love more quickly. The strike was ruining more lives than even management and the colliers knew about.

Amy went into the hall. Enyd was still

watching over the boys who were stacking the sacks in the store-room. A bucket of carrots and a knife had been set on the table she usually worked at. She hung up her cloak and made a start.

Enyd saw the last load of vegetables into the store-room, turned the key and locked the door. The carter was sitting at a table drinking tea and talking to Amy.

'Hello, Mr Robinson. We met outside. I'm Enyd Jenkins.'

'Pleased to meet you, Mrs Jenkins.' The carter shook Enyd's hand.

'Are you driving back through Pontypridd, Mr Robinson?' she asked.

'I only wish Pontypridd was as far as I have to go.'

'Could you give me a lift there, please?'

'If you want one, Mrs Jenkins. But it's cold, wet and windy on top of the cart,' he said. 'You can hardly tuck yourself under the covers with the boys in the back. It's filthy from the potatoes.'

'I'll be fine sitting up front with you, Mr Robinson. It won't be the first time I've sat on a cart.'

'I doubt you've sat on one in this weather that often. But if you're determined to travel with us, I'll be leaving as soon as the boys have finished their tea.'

'I'll be ready, Mr Robinson.' Enyd took the key of the store-room to Father Kelly. 'Can you manage without me for the rest of the day, Father? Mr Robinson is going to Pontypridd and has offered me a lift. I've some business there that I've been meaning to attend to.'

'If that business is begging your brother for donations for the kitchen, forget it, Enyd. I've tried. The man would rather give his bones to dogs than to a soup kitchen, even though most of his customers are miners.'

Enyd's brother had inherited the family butcher's in Pontypridd. It was common knowledge that he and Enyd hadn't spoken since she had moved to Tonypandy with the Watkins.

'With all respect, Father, you're not his sister.' She buttoned the cuffs on her blouse.

'You're wasting your time, Enyd, and you'll catch your death of cold on that cart,' he called after her.

The only reply he had was, 'I'll see you tomorrow morning, Father.' Enyd stopped to kiss Amy goodbye, before following the carter and his boys out of the door.

'Is there anywhere special you want to go to in Pontypridd?' Fred Robinson asked Enyd when they reached the end of Mill Street. Ahead was Taff Street and the centre of town.

'Here will be fine, Mr Robinson. I know Father Kelly will write to the farmers, but please thank them from the colliers' wives in Tonypandy for their donation of vegetables .'

'I've never been thanked so much for doing so little, Mrs Jenkins. I'll pass your message on.' He pulled his scarf over his mouth to protect his face from the rain that had soaked his cap and collar.

Enyd gripped the side of the cart and climbed down on to the pavement. Her legs and arms were numb, stiff with cold, and her cloak was soaked. When she began to walk she discovered that her skirt, petticoats, cardigan and blouse were also wet through.

'Hope you get a ride back, Mrs Jenkins.' Fred cracked the reins and his shire horses moved on.

Enyd looked around. She knew exactly where she wanted to go. She also didn't want to risk anyone who knew her seeing her go there. She pulled her bonnet down low and her scarf high so it covered the lower part of her face. She turned left out of Mill Street. Her brother's butcher's shop was in Broadway in the opposite direction. But she had no wish to see him. She walked along Taff Street and turned left again into Market Square.

The Colliery Company had their offices in the square. She knew that Arnold Craggs worked there for an hour or two most mornings before going to the best hotel in town, the New Inn, for lunch. She reached the door and straightened her cloak. There were mud splashes on the left-hand side where it had hung over the cart, but there was nothing she could do about it. Rubbing damp mud only drove it deeper into the cloth.

She tucked her wet hair beneath her bonnet and wiped her face with her wet woollen gloves. Only then did she press the bell on the door.

A young man dressed in a suit, winged collar and bow tie opened the door. He looked down at Enyd from the height of the doorstep. The expression on his face told Enyd that he saw everything: her wet clothes and the dirt on her cloak that meant she'd travelled by cart, not train or bus.

'Yes?'

Enyd raised her eyes and met his glare. 'I'm here to see Mr Arnold Craggs.'

'Have you an appointment?' He moved back. She sensed he was preparing to close the door in her face.

'No, but he will see me, if you give him my name. Enyd Lewis.'

'Mr Craggs has left orders that he is not to be disturbed.'

'Give him this.' Enyd couldn't bring herself to use the word please to the man. She opened her handbag and handed the clerk her red leather jewellery box. He opened it. 'Is this Mr Craggs's property?'

'Just give it to him.'

'Are you returning it to him after it was stolen?'

'Just give it to him, please,' she repeated.

'Your name again?'

'Enyd Lewis.' Enyd summoned her courage. 'Mr Craggs won't thank you for keeping me waiting.'

'Wait here.' The clerk opened the door wide enough to allow Enyd inside. Enyd stood, her clothes dripping water onto the tiled floor. A few minutes later the clerk came back. 'Mr Craggs will see you.' He led the way up two flights of stairs and opened a door. Enyd entered the room and the clerk closed the door behind her.

The office couldn't have been more different from a miner's cottage. It was as large as Enyd's parlour, hall, passage and kitchen combined. One wall had wide windows that overlooked Market Square. A fire had been banked up in a vast marble fireplace. The walls were papered in gold. The furniture was mahogany. Arnold Craggs sat behind a massive, leather-topped desk that almost filled the room.

The years had been kind to him. He was still slim and his eyes were as blue as Enyd remembered. Only his hair had changed. There was more silver than blond in the strands that fell over his forehead. He rose to his feet when she entered and pointed to an armchair next to the fire.

'Hello, Enyd. It's good to see you. Please, sit down.'

'I'm wet. I'd ruin your chair.'

'I don't mind.'

'I would. I didn't come here to spoil your furniture.'

'I've been hoping that you would visit me for years. Why now? After all this time?'

'Because a young Irishman called Thomas Kelly needs help. You were the only person I could think of who might be able to do something for him.'

Chapter Nine

'I wouldn't go out there, if I were you, boy,' Constable Davies advised Tom Kelly. Tom had left the cell where he had slept for most of the morning and was walking towards the front door of the police station.

'I'm a free man, aren't I?' Tom asked.

'You haven't been arrested. But you're only as free as the colliery company lets you be. Or do you need reminding that you've signed on with them?' Huw Davies asked.

'After what happened last night, I don't need reminding.'

'I've no doubt they'll send someone to pick you up as soon as the streets are safe.' Huw sat behind a large desk.

'I overheard Sergeant Martin tell one of the officers that most of the colliers have gone back to the picket lines.' Tom buttoned his loose tweed jacket and turned up his collar.

'Most, not all,' Huw said. 'You're a known blackleg. If a collier recognises you, you're likely to get the same treatment the others had last night. We heard this morning that none of them will be fit for work for at least a month.'

'The colliery company got more than it expected when it took them on.' Gwyn Jenkins, another local constable commented. 'Medically unfit blacklegs and big hospital bills. I wouldn't like to be in Shipton's shoes. Where were he and the other duty constable when the colliers took the blacklegs out of the stables?'

'He's explaining that to the sergeant and Arnold Craggs' agent now.' Huw Davies turned to Tom. 'Why don't you forget about going to see your uncle for a day or two? If you return to your cell, you can have a lie down. I'll bring you a nice cup of tea.'

'I've had enough of lying down.'

'It's better than getting beaten up.'

Tom grinned. 'I've proved I can run fast.'

Huw Davies refused to smile. 'It might not be fast enough next time, boy.'

'Ten minutes. That's all it'll take for me to walk around the corner, talk to my uncle and tell him I'm all right.'

'Sergeant Martin spoke to Father Kelly this morning. He told him you were in one piece then.'

'I have a letter to give him. A personal letter.' Tom clutched the folded paper in his pocket. He'd begged a sheet of paper and a pencil from one of the constables that morning and had written a note to Amy. He had no envelope, but he trusted his uncle to deliver it unread. 'You can't stop me going, can you?'

'No.' Huw Davies saw that Tom was determined to leave. 'But if you have to go, at least let me look outside to make sure there are no colliers watching the entrance.' He went to the door.

'Is the street clear?' Tom asked.

'At the moment, but be quick. Someone from the colliery company could come to fetch you any minute.'

'That's not likely,' Gwyn Jenkins said. 'They need more than one lucky blackleg who escaped a hanging and a beating to keep the colliery going.'

'Tom, be careful.' Huw Davies was talking to a closed door. Tom Kelly had gone.

Mark Watkins had spent all morning standing across the road from the soup kitchen. He was cold, wet, hungry and bored, but he forgot his troubles when he saw Tom Kelly come round the corner and run up the hill towards him.

Mark waved his arm. Half a dozen colliers, armed with planks of wood they'd torn from colliery railings, left the lane behind him. They joined Mark, but were careful to stand back, out of sight of anyone climbing the hill. All they had to do was wait.

Arnold Craggs picked up the jewellery box Enyd had given the clerk. He opened it and turned it around on the desk so it faced her.

'It's been years since we last spoke, Enyd. I'm surprised you kept the locket I gave you.'

'You put a picture of yourself in it. It was the only one I had.'

He pressed the catch. The front flew open to reveal a head and shoulders portrait that had been taken of him when he'd been a young man. On the other side was a photograph of a baby. 'I wanted to help you.'

'You did.'

'Not enough.'

'You had a wife. I was young, foolish and wanted to believe in the fairy tale "Happily ever after". We had an affair that resulted in a baby. It's an old story, Arnold. All that needed to be said about it was said years ago.' She picked up the locket, returned it to the jewellery box and closed the lid.

'I've seen Amy,' he murmured. 'She's beautiful. Just as you were at her age.'

'You always knew how to flatter a woman, Arnold. I've never been beautiful. Not even twenty years ago.'

'You were to me, Enyd. I never stopped loving you. Or regretting what might have been.'

Despite refusing a chair earlier, Enyd found herself in one of the guest chairs next to the fireplace. Arnold sat opposite her. Close, but not close enough to touch her.

'You live in the same street as Mary and Jim Watkins. You must have seen a lot of Amy when she growing up.' Arnold sounded envious.

'Mary and Jim Watkins have done a good job of bringing Amy up, Arnold. They wouldn't have been able to look after her as well, without the money you gave them to buy a house in Tonypandy. Or the job you organised for Jim in the Glamorgan Colliery.'

'They never found out that I gave them the money to buy the house?'

'No. As you and your solicitor planned,

they think Jim's great-uncle left money and no will. They were suspicious, but Jim's great-uncle never married and was thought to be a miser. That helped.'

'And your house?'

'I told everyone that my brother bought me out of my share of the family butcher's.'

'Your brother robbed you.'

Enyd shrugged. 'I brought disgrace on the family.'

'Jim never found out that I pulled strings to get him the job in the Glamorgan?'

'No.'

'You married?'

'A good man who believes Amy is Mary and Jim's child.' Enyd held her hands out to the fire and her woollen gloves began to steam. 'He wouldn't have married me if he'd any idea of the truth.'

'Who would have thought it possible that you could silence so many gossips by moving a few miles?'

'People in Pontypridd forgot about me when I moved to Tonypandy with Mary and Jim. I was careful never to leave Mary and Jim's house without my cloak until after Amy was born. People in Tonypandy never doubted Mary when she said Amy was her child.'

'Gwilym Jenkins isn't that good a man, Enyd. He's a strike leader,' Arnold said.

'You know the name of the man I married?' She looked at him in surprise.

'Do you think that I could forget about you and Amy? She is my only child, Enyd.'

'You have no children, Arnold.'

He clenched his fists. 'Yes I do,' he cried.

'None you can own.'

'Does Amy know who her parents are?'

'Yes, Arnold. Mary and Jim Watkins are Amy's parents. They nursed her when she was a baby. They looked after her when she caught measles, mumps and chicken-pox. They fed her, cared for her and gave her all the love and attention she could ever want.'

'If you'd given me the chance I would have loved her, Enyd.'

'As your bastard child?'

'I would have bought the two of you a fine house, not a miner's cottage, Enyd.'

'A miner's cottage was all I would take.'

'As if I needed reminding. I would have given you money and all the clothes and jewellery you and Amy wanted. I would have paid for Amy to go to private school.'

'Where she would have been called a bastard, and I would have been called your mistress, by people who wanted to be kind. The unkind ones would have called me whore.'

'You were never a whore, Enyd.'

'It's what the world would have called me if they had found out about Amy. But thanks to Mary and Jim Watkins, and your money, Amy's and my life turned out differently.'

'Can't we at least be friends, Enyd?'

'No, Arnold. We can never be friends. I told you that twenty years ago and it's truer now than it was then. I asked you about Thomas Kelly. Do you know him?'

'One of our agents told me he'd signed up Father Kelly's nephew in Ireland.'

'Tear up the papers Tom signed, Arnold. Your agents tricked him. He's no blackleg.'

'What's Thomas Kelly to you?' He thought for a moment. 'Of course, you work in Father Kelly's kitchen. He sent you here to beg for his nephew, didn't he?'

'Father Kelly doesn't know I'm here. No one does, except you and the clerk who showed me in.'

'I'm sorry he was rude to you. He's a snob but good at his job, which is why I employ him.'

'The colliers see the strike as a war, Arnold. We're on different sides. Amy Watkins and Tom

Kelly are caught in the middle.' Enyd glanced at the clock above Arnold's desk. It was already twelve o'clock. She didn't have much time to find a ride back to Tonypandy and get there before Gwilym left the picket line.

'Amy knows Tom?'

'She loves him.'

'And Jim Watkins approves?'

'No, he doesn't. He'll disown Amy if he finds out about them. I've seen Tom and Amy together, Arnold. It's hopeless to try and separate them. They're in love. Just as ...' She fell silent.

'We were,' he finished for her.

'You'll tear up Tom Kelly's contract?' she pleaded.

'I won't make promises I can't keep, Enyd. I did that once before when I told a young girl I'd leave my wife and take care of her. All I really did was hurt the only woman I ever loved.'

Enyd looked at him for a moment, storing his face in her memory. 'I know you'll try, Arnold. I've done what I came here to do. I have to go to the market and look for a cart that's going back to Tonypandy.'

'I'll hire a cab for you.'

She burst out laughing. 'Oh no you won't. Can you imagine what people would say if they saw the wife of a striking miner, riding into Tonypandy in style? I'd never live it down. Gwilym wouldn't understand the waste of money. And I certainly couldn't tell him where it came from.'

'At least let me give you the train fare.'

'No, for the same reason. I'd have to explain to Gwilym where I got it.'

Arnold took his wallet from his pocket and opened it. He removed two ten-pound notes. 'Then give these to Father Kelly for his soup kitchen.'

'Father Kelly wouldn't take them from you.'

'You wouldn't have to tell him where they came from.'

'I couldn't lie. You want to donate, Arnold, do it without saying who you are, anonymously.'

'I already do.' He left his desk and went to the door.

'If you have any feelings for Amy, Arnold, help her and Tom. But promise me, one thing. Don't ever tell her who you are.'

'And that's all you'll take from me, Enyd. A promise?'

'It is.'

'You have it.'

She kissed his cheek. 'Goodbye, Arnold.'

Chapter Ten

Tom lay on his back on the pavement. He hadn't seen the blow that felled him. It came from behind and had been too hard to have come from a fist. There was a loud ringing in his ears, but it wasn't loud enough to drown out Mark's voice.

'You bastard, blackleg. We'll teach you to stay away from decent girls. You say one more word to my sister and I'll kill you.'

Tom saw Mark's boot. A crack sounded in the cold air. Terrible pains burned through his left arm and into his chest. Boots and wooden staves rained down on him. He curled into a tight ball and lifted his arms in an attempt to protect his head.

Screams tore through the air. He only recognised them as his when the pain was so great he could no longer cry out.

A familiar Irish voice rose above the curses of the men who were beating him.

'Dear God, boys. What's going on here? Stop it. Stop it.'

Tom tried to focus on his uncle. He saw his black cassock, and his face as he crouched on the ground beside him.

'Tom, lad. Oh Tom.'

Tom heard Amy scream his name. He heard the sound of running feet, small, light feet. The voice drew closer.

'Mark, what have you done? You brute.'

'Amy.' He tried to say her name, but the noise he made didn't make any sense. He tried again. 'Amy.' Then he plunged into merciful, pain-numbing darkness.

'Amy, love, you have to let the men take Tom to hospital. Father Kelly will go with him.' Realizing that Amy hadn't heard a word she'd said, Betty Morgan looked for help. 'Where's Enyd Jenkins? She and Amy are close.'

'She went to Pontypridd.' Father Kelly cradled Tom's bloody head in his lap.

'All Tom did was talk to me, Mark,' Amy shouted. 'Do you hear? All he did was talk to me.'

Betty and two of the other ladies held Amy back when she closed her fists.

'At last, the ambulance.' Father Kelly breathed in relief when he saw the horses galloping up the hill.

'And the police.' Mark shouted. 'Run, boys.'

The strikers ran off. Three of them headed for the mountain, Mark and two others disappeared down a side street.

Amy watched the driver of the ambulance and his mate load Tom on to a stretcher.

'It's just as well he's out of it,' the driver said to Father Kelly. 'He wouldn't be able to stand the pain otherwise.'

'He will be all right, won't he?' Amy begged.

The driver looked at her before glancing at his mate and Father Kelly.

'He will be all right. He has to be.' She slipped through Betty's grasp and ran to the stretcher.

'The doctors will do all they can, Amy.' Father Kelly hugged her. 'All you can do now is let us get him to them quickly, so they can do their job.'

Betty Morgan wrapped her arm around Amy and called to one of the boys who'd been watching the scene.

'Run down to the picket line outside the Glamorgan colliery and tell Mr Ned Morgan and Mr Jim Watkins they're needed up here. As quickly as they can get here.'

Jim Watkins faced his son and daughter across

the cold hearth in their kitchen. 'I want the truth, from both of you. Mark why did you beat Tom Kelly?'

'Because he's a blackleg.'

'I hate blacklegs as much as the next miner. But you know my views on violence.'

Mark stared at Amy. 'I saw Amy kissing him.'

Jim Watkins turned to his daughter. 'When?'

'When I was coming back from the Ty Bach last night. I'd been asleep and had to get up. They were outside the front door and they were kissing.'

'Is this true?' Jim demanded of Amy.

Amy couldn't tell a lie. 'Yes.'

Jim raised his voice. 'He's a blackleg.'

'I love him,' she said simply.

Jim clenched and unclenched his fists. He'd never hit Amy. But she knew it was the closest he'd come to it.

'Go to your room, Amy. You don't leave this house. Not to go to the soup kitchen or anywhere else. Get upstairs girl.'

Amy walked through the door and climbed the stairs.

The doctor left the operating theatre and

walked down the corridor. Father Kelly was sitting in the bleak, cold, tiled waiting room. The priest rose when he saw the doctor.

The doctor shook his head. 'It's bad, Father. We had to operate. One of his ribs splintered and pierced his lung. His right arm's broken in three places, his left in two. Worst of all is the fracture to his skull.'

'He will recover?' The priest whispered the question as though he were praying.

'I don't want to give you any false hope, Father. I've never seen a man recover from injuries as bad as his. I advise you to start looking for a burial plot. I suggest one that's well away from where the colliers bury their dead.'

Amy heard the loud knock at the door and went to the top of stairs. Her mother opened the door. Sergeant Martin was on the doorstep.

'Is Mark here, Mrs Watkins?'

Mary lifted her apron to her eyes and wiped them. 'In the kitchen with his father.'

'I have to see him.'

Mary stood aside. 'He's expecting you.'

Amy didn't leave the landing. She heard voices in the kitchen. Her father, Mark and the sergeant were speaking too low for her to hear what they were saying. Ten minutes later the sergeant led Mark out. Her father followed them as far as the front door. He looked up and saw her watching.

'You don't have to tell me this is all my fault.' Her voice was hoarse, blurred with unshed tears.

'Tom Kelly is dying, and half the people in the soup kitchen saw Mark and the others beat him to a pulp.'

Amy started down the stairs.

'Go back to your room, Amy.' There was no anger, only sorrow, in Jim's voice.

'I have to see Tom.'

'He's dying, Amy, too ill to see anyone. The doctor wouldn't even let Father Kelly see him.'

Amy crept back into her bedroom and closed the door. She lay on her bed and wept. She had seen her beloved brother beat the man she loved to death. Life simply wasn't worth living any more.

'I thought you were lucky when you escaped the round up of blacklegs from the stables of the White Hart. Then, when Mark Watkins and his boys gave you thrashing, I thought you weren't that lucky. Now I think you have more lives than a cat.' Sergeant Martin stood at the foot of Tom Kelly's bed in the men's ward of the local hospital.

'We Kellys are a tough breed,' Tom croaked. A kick to his neck had bruised his throat and affected his speech.

'Constable Davies tells me that you refuse to press charges against Mark Watkins and the other men who attacked you?'

'If I'd ever had a job worth fighting for, I would have done the same as them.'

'You still want to go to America?'

'Yes.'

'Good idea. Get as far away from the Rhondda as you can. The doctor says you'll need to take things easy for a few months. But you'll be able to leave hospital and travel in a month's time.'

'My uncle wants me to stay with him for a while. But –' A coughing fit stopped Tom from saying more.

'You'd rather not make life any more difficult for him than you already have?' the sergeant guessed.

Tom nodded.

Sergeant Martin pulled a chair close to the bed, sat down and lowered his voice. 'I have a message for you from someone who will pay your fare to Southampton, your lodging there and your sea ticket to America? All you have to do is get in the cab they send for you when you leave hospital.'

'What about the contract I signed with the colliery company?'

Sergeant Martin handed him an envelope. Tom opened it. Inside was the paper he'd signed in Ireland.

'I suggest you tear it up.'

'Why are you helping me?'

'I'm only the messenger boy.'

'Who are you working for?'

'I can't tell you.'

'How is Amy Watkins?'

'Her father has her locked up. Or so I've heard. What do I tell your helper? Should he go ahead and make the arrangements?'

Tom thought of his uncle. He'd hurt him and his place in Tonypandy enough. But did this offer come from the strikers? Wasn't one beating enough? Were they determined to kill him?

If he left Tonypandy, would Amy's father set her free? Her freedom was worth his life.

'You won't tell me who is helping me?'

'If I did, my life would be worth even less than yours.'

Tom fell back on his pillow. 'Tell whoever it is thank you, and to go ahead and make the arrangements.'

A month later Enyd checked the contents of the envelope that had been delivered by hand to her house after Gwilym had left for the picket line. Forty pounds in gold sovereigns. Two first-class train tickets from Pontypridd to Southampton. A banker's draft in the name of Thomas Kelly for one thousand pounds. Another banker's draft in the name of Amy Watkins for one thousand pounds. Two saloon class tickets for a White Star Liner due to leave Southampton for New York in April. And a receipt showing payment for a hotel suite in Southampton until April.

There was also an envelope addressed to her. She opened it and took out a sheet of paper. The note wasn't signed and there was only one line of writing.

Wish the lovers Bon Voyage and a long and happy life.

'I need Amy to help me carry the loaves to the soup kitchen, Mary,' Enyd said. 'You and Jim can't keep her locked up here for ever. It's inhuman.'

Mary carried on peeling the potatoes and carrots she had bought with the boys' strike pay. She wished she could have bought some meat to go with them. 'Jim doesn't want Amy going near Father Kelly or his soup kitchen.'

'Father Kelly is the same man he always was. Tom Kelly has been in hospital for weeks and is likely to remain there for some time. There's no danger of Amy seeing him. And Jim needs to remember that Mark and his friends would be facing charges for beating Tom Kelly half to death, if Tom hadn't insisted that the police drop the case.'

Mary looked at Amy. She'd grown even thinner and paler in the six weeks her father had kept her locked in the house.

'You be back in this house by four. And no telling your father I let you go, or neither of us will hear the end of it.'

'Yes, Mam.'

'It's freezing out there, Amy. I'd get a thicker cardigan if I were you.' Enyd slipped her hand into Amy's. It was ice cold. But there were also two slips of paper hidden in her fingers. Amy pocketed the notes.

'I'll run upstairs and get one, Auntie Enyd.'

The first piece of paper Amy unfolded had been torn from a small notebook. There were bloodstains on the edge, and it was so crumpled it took her a full minute to read it.

Dear Amy,
I'm sorry for all the trouble I caused you. I love you. I always will but after what's happened I know there is no hope for us. Forget me. I will love you for ever,
Tom.

The next was written on thick watermarked paper in hand-writing she didn't recognise.

If you want to go to America with Tom Kelly, get in the cab.

It was unsigned. Amy's first thought was that it was a trick. Then she wondered why anyone would do such a thing. On impulse, she picked up her toffee tin and slipped it into the pocket of her cardigan. She pulled another sweater on top of the one she was wearing, ran down the stairs and picked up the cloak. She slipped it over her shoulders and went into the kitchen. Her mother was still peeling carrots. She hugged and kissed her.

Mary pushed her away. 'What's all this?

You're only going to the soup kitchen for a couple of hours.'

'I wanted to say thank you and explain about Tom. I couldn't help myself, Mam. I love him.'

Mary carried on angrily peeling. 'I know.'

Amy went to the front door and hung up the cloak before leaving the house. Her mother would need it.

The cab was waiting where Sergeant Martin had told Enyd it would be, outside the Empire Theatre. Anyone seeing it would assume it had been hired by an actor or a manager who had the money to pay the fare.

Amy climbed inside and pulled down the window. 'Auntie Enyd?'

'Close the window and sit back, Amy. Don't risk being seen. The next stop is the hospital. Go with God,' Enyd whispered as the cab drove away.

On April 13th 1912, four envelopes were delivered to four addresses in Wales. Inside each was a photograph of Mr and Mrs Thomas Kelly boarding the newest steamer of the White Star Line. It had sailed out of Southampton on April 10th. The photographs had been ordered and paid for in advance by a firm of solicitors on behalf of a client whose name was kept secret.

Arnold Craggs looked at his copy of the photograph for a long time before locking it into a drawer in his desk.

Father Kelly made the sign of the cross over his, and said a prayer for a long and happy married life for Mr and Mrs Thomas Kelly.

Mary Watkins cried when she saw it. She placed it on the mantlepiece in the kitchen. It stood next to the tin where she kept all the letters Amy had written to her since she had walked out of the house for the last time.

Jim Watkins wondered where Thomas Kelly had found the money to dress himself and his wife so well and to buy their tickets to New York. He didn't say a word to Mary, but he was pleased that Amy looked happy.

Mark Watkins felt guilty and ashamed whenever he looked at the photograph.

Mathew and Jack Watkins noticed that Tom Kelly's injuries had healed well.

Gwilym Jenkins was annoyed when Enyd cried over the photograph. He watched her mop her tears in a handkerchief.

'The problem with you Enyd is, because you've had no children of your own to fuss over, you've ended up taking too much interest in other people's.'

Quick Reads

Books in the Quick Reads series

101 Ways to get your Child to Read	Patience Thomson
All These Lonely People	Gervase Phinn
Black-Eyed Devils	Catrin Collier
The Cave	Kate Mosse
Chickenfeed	Minette Walters
Cleanskin	Val McDermid
A Cool Head	Ian Rankin
Danny Wallace and the Centre of the Universe	Danny Wallace
The Dare	John Boyne
Doctor Who: I Am a Dalek	Gareth Roberts
Doctor Who: Made of Steel	Terrance Dicks
Doctor Who: Revenge of the Judoon	Terrance Dicks
Doctor Who: The Sontaran Games	Jacqueline Rayner
Dragons' Den: Your Road to Success	
A Dream Come True	Maureen Lee
Girl on the Platform	Josephine Cox
The Grey Man	Andy McNab
The Hardest Test	Scott Quinnell
Hell Island	Matthew Reilly
How to Change Your Life in 7 Steps	John Bird
Humble Pie	Gordon Ramsay
Life's New Hurdles	Colin Jackson
Lily	Adèle Geras
One Good Turn	Chris Ryan
RaW Voices: True Stories of Hardship	Vanessa Feltz
Reaching for the Stars	Lola Jaye
Reading My Arse!	Ricky Tomlinson
Star Sullivan	Maeve Binchy
The Sun Book of Short Stories	
Survive the Worst and Aim for the Best	Kerry Katona
The 10 Keys to Success	John Bird
The Tannery	Sherrie Hewson
Twenty Tales from the War Zone	John Simpson

Quick Reads

Pick up a book today

Quick Reads are bite-sized books by bestselling writers and well-known personalities for people who want a short, fast-paced read. They are designed to be read and enjoyed by avid readers and by people who never had or who have lost the reading habit.

Quick Reads are published alongside and in partnership with BBC RaW.

We would like to thank all our partners in the Quick Reads project for their help and support:

Arts Council England
The Department for Innovation, Universities and Skills
NIACE
unionlearn
National Book Tokens
The Vital Link
The Reading Agency
National Literacy Trust
Welsh Books Council
Basic Skills Cymru, Welsh Assembly Government
Wales Accent Press
The Big Plus Scotland
DELNI
NALA

Quick Reads would also like to thank the Department for Innovation, Universities and Skills; Arts Council England and World Book Day for their sponsorship and NIACE for their outreach work.

Quick Reads is a World Book Day initiative.
www.quickreads.org.uk www.worldbookday.com

Quick Reads

The Cave

Kate Mosse

Orion

It is March 1928. Frederick is on holiday in the mountains of south west France. When his car crashes, he goes to a hotel in the nearest village. There is only one other guest, a beautiful young woman called Marie. She tells how, 600 years ago, a war forced the villagers to leave their homes. They hid in a cave but, when the fighting was over, no one came back. Their bodies were never found.

The next day, Marie has gone, and Freddie decides to look for the cave himself. It is a decision he will live to regret...

The Cave is the gripping new adventure from the number-one bestselling author of *Labyrinth* and *Sepulchre*.

Other resources

Free courses are available for anyone who wants to develop their skills. You can attend the courses in your local area. If you'd like to find out more, phone 0800 66 0800.

A list of books for new readers can be found on www.firstchoicebooks.org.uk or at your local library.

Publishers Barrington Stoke (www.barringtonstoke.co.uk), New Island (www.newisland.ie) and Sandstone Press (www.sandstonepress.com) also provide books for new readers.

The BBC runs a reading and writing campaign. See www.bbc.co.uk/raw.

www.quickreads.org.uk www.worldbookday.com